"Hey, Tanner, will you be my daddy?"

Tanner's mouth dropped open in surprise and he felt as though he'd been slugged in the gut.

"Jonah!" Zoë looked at her son as if he'd just slapped her, too.

"Um, what do you mean?" Tanner almost choked on the words. How he wished he could be this boy's father. But that would mean he'd have to be Zoë's husband. And that was impossible under the circumstances.

"For the church's father-son outing. I need a dad to go with me." The boy smiled happily, completely unaware of the consternation his request had caused the adults in the room.

Zoë gave him an apologetic frown. "I'm sorry, Tanner. I didn't know Jonah was going to ask you to do this. He's just a kid and doesn't always think things through before he jumps in with both feet."

Yeah, a cute little kid Tanner had grown to love in spite of his vow never to do so.

Books by Leigh Bale

Love Inspired

The Healing Place
The Forever Family
The Road to Forgiveness
The Forest Ranger's Promise
The Forest Ranger's Husband
The Forest Ranger's Child
Falling for the Forest Ranger

LEIGH BALE

is an author of inspirational romance who has won multiple awards for her work, including the prestigious Golden Heart. She is the daughter of a retired U.S. forest ranger, holds a B.A. in history with distinction and is a member of Phi Kappa Phi Honor Society. She loves working, writing, grandkids, spending time with family, weeding the garden with her dog Sophie and watching the little sagebrush lizards that live in her rock flower beds. She has two married children and lives in Nevada with her professor husband of thirty-one years. Visit her website at www.LeighBale.com.

Falling for the Forest Ranger

Leigh Bale

Love Inspired

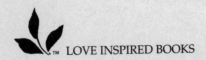 LOVE INSPIRED BOOKS

ISBN-13: 978-0-373-08267-4

FALLING FOR THE FOREST RANGER

When I consider thy heavens,
the work of thy fingers, the moon and the stars,
which thou hast ordained; what is man, that thou
art mindful of him?... Thou madest him to have
dominion over the works of thy hands; thou hast
put all things under his feet... O Lord our Lord,
how excellent is thy name in all the earth!
—*Psalms* 8:3–9

For Steve, the love of my life, my all
and everything. My garden of Eden.

And many thanks to Bruce Smith and Dan Baird,
who actually lived it.

Chapter One

"Jonah, be careful with that!"

Too late. The six-year-old's careless playing had already sent the shopping cart careening across the parking lot, and the boy's little legs couldn't run fast enough to stop it. As the cart slammed into the door of a blue pickup truck parked near the main entrance, a loaf of whole-wheat bread fell from the shopping bags and thumped to the black asphalt. Three oranges and an apple rolled beneath the truck that now bore an impressive four-inch scratch across the side of the door.

Zoë Lawton dropped the sack of potatoes and the package of toilet paper she was carrying and chased after her son. The strap of her handbag slipped off her shoulder and hung around her forearm, hampering her efforts. The purse hit the ground, its contents spilling across the pavement.

This day just kept getting worse.

A tall man stood a few feet away where he'd been placing his own groceries into the back of the truck. In her brief perusal, Zoë caught a glimpse of his firm mouth, piercing brown eyes and a glacial stare that could have coated Death Valley in ice.

"I'm sorry, Mom. I didn't mean to," Jonah wailed.

The culprit stooped beneath the truck, scrambling to pick up two of the oranges. His sparkling blue eyes were filled with remorse. To add insult to injury, he pushed the shopping cart out of his way, gouging another mark across the left front fender of the truck.

"Jonah, stop already!" Zoë clasped her son's hand and pulled him away so he couldn't do any more damage.

"I just wanna help," the boy said.

"I think you've helped enough." The man's deep voice sounded low and angry, like rumbling thunder. He stalked over to stand in front of them, placing his hands on his lean hips as he perused the scratches with an irritated scowl.

Not brown. His eyes were amber, with a dark coppery ring around each of the irises.

Looking up, Jonah's chin trembled. "I'm real sorry, Mister. I didn't mean to."

For a fleeting moment, Zoë saw a flicker of compassion in the man's eyes. Then he raked his fingers through his short, dark hair, showing his frustration. "I just bought this truck three weeks ago."

His growled words showed his annoyance but seemed to be for himself alone. A passing comment that made Zoë feel even worse. If some little kid banged a shopping cart into her new truck, she wouldn't be happy about it, either.

Zoë pasted her most apologetic smile on her face and met the man's gaze. "I'm sorry. I'm going to pay for this. I'll take care of the damage."

He turned and she caught the scent of his spicy cologne, mingled with spearmint. A short lock of sable-brown hair fell over his high forehead, just above one arched brow. Though Zoë was tall for a woman, she had to look up to meet his eyes. Strong, athletic shoulders covered by a black ribbed T-shirt blocked her view of Jonah. The man braced his legs, his muscular thighs sheathed in worn blue jeans. Scuffed cowboy boots topped it all off. A completely masculine man.

And highly annoyed.

As she gathered up the contents of her purse, Zoë wished she'd changed her soiled shirt and faded denims for a clean set of clothes before heading to the grocery store. Having just arrived in town three days earlier, her time had been spent setting up summer child care for Jonah and straightening up the three-bedroom house she'd rented along the bench bordering Bingham River. In spite of the morning rain and May breeze sweeping through the valley, a rivulet of perspiration dampened the back of her neck. She'd worked hard today and felt grungy and exhausted. There'd been no time to fix her hair or apply makeup. Now she felt mortified to be seen looking like a street urchin with a hooligan child. She brushed a hand over her short hair, self-conscious about her bedraggled appearance.

"Just forget about it," the man said with a rasping voice.

"What?" Zoë took Jonah's hand and blinked, trying to concentrate on something besides the man's full mouth and blunt chin.

"I said, let it go. The damage isn't worth bothering with. Besides, every work truck worth a dime has a few good scratches on it." He gave her a half smile that didn't quite reach his eyes.

Did he mean it or was he just trying to get rid of her? Jonah wriggled against her side and she released his hand, thinking he'd stay put this time. She was wrong.

He hurried over and clasped the edge of the truck, jumping up to peer over the side. The rubber soles of his tennis shoes squeaked as he braced his toes against the man's truck to get traction.

"Jonah! Come away from there." She glanced at the man, her cheeks burning like road flares. Now was not a good time for her son to misbehave.

"I just wanted to see what's inside," Jonah said.

"Nothing but sacks of groceries." The man heaved a disgruntled sigh and shook his head at the boy.

"He's normally a well-mannered child. He usually minds me." Zoë rushed to reassure the man, wondering why it mattered so much to her. She hated the thought of this handsome stranger believing she couldn't control her own son.

"I can see that." He pursed his lips, looking skeptical.

"He's just a bit excited. You see, we just moved to town, and he's been helping me get settled in our new home."

"Yeah, hyper kids act that way sometimes."

She stiffened, fighting off bristles of anger. Calling her son *hyper* pinched a nerve in Zoë's composure. "Jonah's not hyper. He's just curious and energetic."

A miniature replica of his deceased father, Jonah was now kicking the tires. She didn't know what she'd do without him. She certainly wouldn't tolerate anyone assigning him a derogatory label.

The man looked doubtful, but she wasn't about to carry this conversation any further. He had a right to be upset, after all.

She dug into her purse, searching for a pen and paper. "I want to pay for the damage. It's the least I can do."

He held up a hand, his expression darkening. "Don't bother. Right now, I just want to get my ice cream home and in the freezer before it melts."

"Oh, I'm sorry." Zoë thought about her own perishables wilting in her shopping cart. She also wanted to get home, if only to get Jonah into a place where he could run around and burn off some energy. With the boy bouncing around the house, she doubted there'd be much relaxation until bedtime. Rather than try to cook dinner, she'd pick up hamburgers at the drive-through on the way. Since their move, Jonah had been wound as tight as a top. If only she could bottle and sell her son's energy, she'd be filthy rich.

"Hey, do you like fish?" Jonah pointed at the rear bumper of the man's truck. Zoë craned her neck to see a blue sticker with two Pacific salmon on it that read Save Our Salmon.

The man didn't move but responded impatiently, "Yeah, I like fish just fine."

Jonah flashed a wide grin. "My mom does, too. She knows *everything* about fish."

The man eyed Zoë as a dubious smile creased the corners of his mouth. "I'll just bet she does. You got a goldfish at home, do you?"

"Yep. How'd you know that?" Jonah screwed his face up in curiosity.

"Just a lucky guess."

"My name's Jonah, like Jonah and the whale. Mom's told me the Bible story over and over. Jonah was disbedient to the Lord, so he got swallowed up into the whale's belly. Only when he pented did the Lord cause the whale to throw him up."

Zoë stared at her son, stunned by his version of the tale. "Dis-o-be-di-ent and re-pen-ted." She enunciated the words slowly for her child.

The man coughed, a suppressed smile twitching his lips. "I've never heard the story told in quite that way."

"I've never been fishing before," Jonah continued. "My daddy died when I was just a baby. Mom promised to take me someday soon, once she learns how."

Zoë shifted her weight, wishing Jonah wouldn't spill their entire life out for a stranger. But she'd raised him to be honest, so she shouldn't be surprised by his candor.

A disbelieving laugh slipped from the

man's corded throat. "You'd better be prepared to hook your own worms. Most women are squeamish about that."

"Not Mom. She can do *anything*."

Jonah's spoken confidence touched Zoë's heart. How she loved her little boy. His enthusiasm for life affirmed for her that there was so much good around her. After Derek, her husband, had died five years earlier, she'd wondered if she'd ever be happy again. But Jonah served as a constant reminder of how much she still had to live for.

"I'll just bet she can." The man's gaze traveled the length of her, as if sizing her up. His disbelieving expression told her what he really thought about her. Which made her feel incompetent and silly. And she wasn't. Not at all.

As a National Marine Fisheries biologist for the federal government, she'd worked hard in a male-dominated field to earn her graduate degree and advance in her career. With Derek's death, she'd been forced to expand her earning base to provide a living for her eleven-month-old baby. With a day job, night classes and a little boy to raise, she'd worked hard to get where she was today. She was used to people, mostly men, telling her she couldn't succeed, but she'd learned to ignore them. Her knowledge certainly wasn't limited to goldfish in a bowl, but she wasn't about to expound on her training and experience in this parking lot.

Not with an irate stranger.

Tanner Bohlman wanted out of this parking lot. Right now. He didn't care that Jonah's mother had a gorgeous smile that lit up her dazzling blue eyes, and he certainly wasn't interested that the lady was trying to give him her name and phone number.

"At least take my contact info in case you change your mind." She thrust a scrap of paper at him with her information scrawled across the top.

Against his better judgment, he glanced at her name. Zoë. Pretty and delicate, just like her. With short, blond hair and a lean, graceful figure.

"Thanks." Without looking down, he crumpled the paper in his fist.

"My goldfish's name is Rocky," the boy said.

"Is that right?" Tanner stepped over to the truck door, desperate to make an escape. Trying to keep from staring at the woman's full mouth and confused frown.

"You ever see some salmon?" the boy persisted.

"Jonah, quit with all the questions." The mother spoke the reprimand softly, but a warning glint filled her eyes.

"Yeah, I've seen a few salmon in my day." Tanner jerked open the door to his truck, trying to ignore the pretty pink flush of color highlighting the woman's cheeks. He didn't want to make small talk with them. He had to leave. Had to get out of here now.

"Mom's gonna take me fishing for trout," Jonah persisted.

"Good for you." He stepped up into the

driver's seat but couldn't slam the door. The kid was in the way.

"Come on, Jonah." The woman pulled her son back, then glanced at Tanner. "Be sure to let me know if you change your mind about the repairs."

Tanner shook his head. "Thanks, but I won't be calling you."

Not ever. The last thing he wanted in his life was another woman, even if her cute little son had accidentally bashed a couple of scratches into the side of his truck. After what his former fiancée had done to him two years earlier, Tanner wouldn't take the chance of falling for another woman ever again. It hurt too much.

He paused, tossing a quick glimpse at Jonah. "You stay back with your mom, now. I don't want to run over you when I back out."

Taking the cue, Zoë gripped the little guy's hand, tugging him out of the way. Satisfied that the boy was safe, Tanner slid the key into the ignition and started the engine. He paused just a moment, giving Zoë time to retrieve her potatoes and the wayward cart. Watching her struggle between holding onto her son's hand and maneuvering the weight of the heavy cart, Tanner almost hopped out to help her.

Almost.

He resisted the urge, giving her time to move aside so he could drive away. He didn't like being rude but figured it was for the best. He just couldn't reciprocate her pleasant mood.

A twinge of regret tightened in his gut when he saw that she'd replaced her apologetic smile with a glare of disapproval. Under the circumstances, she'd tried to be as nice as possible. From what the kid had said, she wasn't married, and a boy like Jonah was bound to be a handful for a woman on her own.

But what had happened to Jonah's father?

Tanner couldn't help wondering. According to Jonah, the man had died. Tanner reminded himself that it wasn't his business.

He didn't like being so curt. But being friendly would only lead to him looking at that scrap of paper she'd given him. Then he'd be tempted to call her. And he wouldn't. Couldn't.

Checking his rearview mirror, he saw that she was still standing there, holding her purse and Jonah's hand, watching Tanner pull out of the parking lot. As he turned the corner and drove away, he forced himself not to look back again.

When he reached the first stoplight, he blew out a harsh breath, his pulse settling back to a normal beat.

He still remembered the color of her eyes. Electric blue, with a subtle midnight ring around each iris. Yeah, he'd noticed, in spite of her little boy's constant chatter and his desire not to like either of them. But noticing that a woman was attractive didn't mean he had to act on it.

As he navigated through traffic and headed toward his lonely apartment on the south side of town, he tossed the crumpled piece of paper she'd given him on the floor. He'd throw it away when he got home. Holding it served as a reminder of how lonely he was.

That couldn't be helped. Better to be lonely than to lose someone else he loved. First his parents, then his grandparents, then his fiancée. He'd been alone most of his life. He liked his solitude and doing what he wanted.

Sometimes.

Tanner shook his head, trying to clear the painful memories surging through his mind. Cheryl telling him she loved him. Hugging him tight. Smiling so sweetly. And then, when she'd broken off their engagement, her sneer of contempt. She'd claimed she'd never loved him or his line of work. Not really. She'd only tolerated all their trips into the mountains. All the fishing excursions and hikes. Waiting until someone better came along.

That someone had been Tanner's best childhood friend.

Ex-best friend now. The hurt of Cheryl's betrayal sank deep into Tanner's heart, like a barbed fishhook. And every time he thought about them, it ripped his heart anew.

Tanner flipped on the turning signal and heaved a giant sigh. It was better to remain a bachelor and throw himself into his work instead. Much more rewarding and something he had control over. Being alone suited him just fine. Then he'd have no one to insist he do things her way. No one to destroy his relationship with his best friend.

No one to love.

Bah! He didn't need love to feel complete or to lead a full, happy life. He'd finally begun to make peace with his past. He'd focused on building his career, which had paid off. He'd recently been promoted as the Fisheries and Wildlife staff officer over the Steelhead National Forest. It kept him plenty busy. In fact, his career was his life.

No, Tanner didn't have the time or the desire to complicate his solitary existence with another superficial romance. Especially with someone like Zoë. The widow came packing baggage. A cute, precocious little troublemaker named Jonah.

As Tanner pulled into his driveway and killed the motor, he realized he had everything he needed. A good education, a comfortable place to live, a challenging career and a few coworkers to hang out with once in a while.

Stepping out of the truck, he glanced back at the wad of paper lying on top of the floor mat. Against his better judgment, he reached inside, picked it up...and tucked it inside his pants pocket.

Chapter Two

No, it couldn't be. It just couldn't.

Tanner Bohlman stared across the conference room in the Steelhead National Forest supervisor's office, unable to believe his eyes. Striding through the door wearing a violet-colored skirt and matching jacket was the woman from the parking lot.

The very same.

It'd been a week since her son had creamed his new truck with a shopping cart. Even with her now wearing makeup and a business suit, he couldn't mistake the apologetic mother who'd offered to pay for repairs to his truck. Zoë was her name.

As much as he'd tried, he couldn't seem to forget it.

Instead of flat and tired-looking, as it'd been that day in the parking lot, her short blond hair had been given a sassy style, spiked slightly in the back with gel. Her pretty mouth shimmered with pink lipstick, her blue eyes accented with a subtle hint of mascara, liner and shadow. Her pale skin showed a healthy glow, her high cheekbones dusted with a hint of blush.

Gary Drummond, the watershed specialist sitting next to Tanner, whistled low beneath his breath. "That's the new marine biologist? I think I'm gonna like her."

"Yeah, me, too," agreed Ron Parker, one of Tanner's fishery biologists.

Both men were married, but you didn't have to be single to appreciate an attractive woman. Tanner admitted silently to himself they were both right. What a looker!

As she shook the forest supervisor's hand and smiled, Tanner remembered the color of her eyes. A vivid shade of blue.

Tanner tried to imagine this feminine woman dressed in hip waders, toddling out into the middle of a stream to take water samples. How could she be the new marine biologist? Where did she think the fish lived? In a high-rise office building?

Not likely.

Right now, Tanner was afraid to breathe too deeply for fear of soiling her pristine business suit. All the other marine biologists he'd ever met before wore blue jeans, tennis shoes or boots, a plain shirt they didn't care about getting dirty and not a hint of makeup, much less a carefully styled hairdo. Of course, he'd never worked with a female marine biologist before.

Until today.

A series of business meetings that morning might account for her professional attire. But why would the National Marine Fisheries Service send this little scrap of lace to the wilds of Idaho to work? Tanner wondered if she even knew how to swim, much less how to help solve their fishery problems. He wasn't about to play nurse-maid to a marine biologist who might be afraid of rumpling her silk blouse.

"Hey, everyone. This is Zoë Lawton." Chuck Daniels, the forest supervisor and Tanner's boss, smiled expectantly as he made the introductions.

"Hi, there," Gary called with a wave of his hand.

"Glad to meet you." Ron grinned like a fool.

Tanner just nodded, biting his tongue to keep from speaking. He didn't trust his voice right now. Instead, he mechanically stood and held out his hand, highly conscious of her soft, manicured fingers as they tightened around his...and the moment she met his gaze and recognized him, too.

"Oh!" she said.

Just *Oh!* Nothing more.

"Do you two know each other?" Chuck asked, glancing between them.

Tanner spoke up fast. "No, we don't."

Zoë. Even her name sounded exotic.

And too fragile to be traipsing around the untamed Idaho river systems. Her name suited her. Sweet and feminine. But those weren't the traits she'd need once he took her up on the mountain to view the various creeks and streams connecting to Bingham River. Tanner wasn't certain, but he figured if a bear attacked her, she could use one of her spiked heels as a weapon. That was just about the only useful, practical aspect he could spot in her outfit.

"But we've met before." Zoë withdrew her hand and gave him an uncertain smile. "I'm sorry again for what happened. I haven't heard from you, so I guess you haven't changed your mind about letting me pay for the damage."

"That's right." He turned and moved around the room, taking a seat on the opposite side of the wide oak table.

She smelled even better than she looked. Like bottled springtime.

As the Fisheries and Wildlife staff officer, Tanner had been assigned the task of giving this woman a tour of Bingham

River and its tributaries. Which would take all summer long. He had to cooperate with her in any way he could.

What rotten luck.

"Why don't we get started?" Tanner glanced at Ron, trying not to sound irritable. The fact that Ron gave him a worried look told Tanner that he'd failed in that endeavor.

"Right." Ron grabbed the overhead clicker. With a punch of his finger, he brought up the first slide to the Power-Point presentation he'd been asked to prepare. A brief overview of the Steelhead National Forest and the fishery problems they were dealing with.

"Will you get the lights, Chuck?" Tanner called over his shoulder.

A click sounded and the room went dim. Tanner focused on the screen at the front of the table, glad to have an excuse to take his eyes off Zoë.

The first slide showed a brilliant picture of Bingham River, the rushing waters bordered by willows, sedges and Kentucky bluegrass.

With each slide, Ron narrated in an overly loud voice. "The elevations of Bingham River range from nine hundred to over five thousand feet. The river and its tributaries are home to numerous animal species, but our focus today will be on the steelhead, bull trout and Chinook salmon. All these fish are on the endangered-species list."

"Don't you have a serious problem with the sockeye, too?" Zoë asked.

Ron's expression wilted along with his confidence. "Um, yes, and sockeye, too. But the only population of sockeye is located at Redfish Lake in the upper Salmon River basin."

"Yes, I'd heard that. But I'm hoping we can work on introducing them to the Bingham River arena."

Tanner interceded, trying not to sound defensive. "We're already working on that. In fact, Ron's done some great work with the Sawtooth Hatchery to help establish the sockeye in Bingham River by using Clear Lake at its head."

Ron showed a broad smile of gratitude for the praise.

"I see. And how many hatcheries do you have?" Zoë asked.

"There are twenty-one salmon and steelhead hatcheries owned or operated by the Service."

The Service was short for the *U.S. Fish and Wildlife Service.*

"Okay, good. Thank you." Zoë turned her serene gaze back to the screen, not seeming ruffled in the least. In fact, she seemed genuinely interested in what they were saying.

And that's when Tanner had an inkling that she wasn't here as some sort of practical joke. She was just doing her job. He'd seen her résumé, which indicated an educated, qualified professional. Maybe he should reserve judgment until he saw what she was capable of.

A picture of Grand Coulee Dam flashed across the screen. A monolith of concrete and steel, the dam stood 550 feet tall. "Large hydroelectric dams and floodgates along the Columbia River have completely blocked the water, so fish can't swim upstream to spawn."

The biologist brought up another slide of the now-abandoned Moses Mine, located ninety miles outside of town. "Tailings from copper mines have poisoned the creeks. It's taken thousands of dollars and decades of work to clean up the mess, and we still don't have it cleaned up. Every time we have another flooding rain, it just brings the poisons back into the creekbeds."

Ron pressed the button again. Another slide of dozens of salmon lying dead across a local farmer's potato field appeared. "Water diversion for irrigation causes numerous problems. Without screens, fish get lost and bypass the canal, ending up in irrigation ditches with nowhere to go. Irrigation usage lowers the water level in creeks, so fish can't swim upstream. With less water, the temperature increases to critical levels. Pollutants become more concentrated. All these things kill off fish fry and smolt by the thousands."

Zoë shook her head, her lips pursed in disgust.

A slide showing a barren mountain once populated by tall ponderosa pine flickered overhead and Ron continued his dialogue. "Many logging operations have been allowed to overharvest trees in some areas, causing massive erosion into the streams."

Ron's last slide showed several red Angus cows standing in the middle of a stream while their owner sat on his horse on the edge of the bank and looked on. "Ranchers allow their cattle to roam freely along the creekbeds, denuding vegetation from the stream banks as well as stomping on the fragile redds."

Ron clicked off the presentation. "That's it."

Tanner nodded at Chuck to turn the lights back on. "And, of course, wildfire also creates an environment for erosion, though we've been taking precautions to help alleviate the possibility of wildfires."

Zoë's chair creaked as she sat back. "But the environment seems to recover more quickly from wildfire erosion than it does from timber-harvest erosion."

"That's correct, Ms. Lawton," Tanner agreed, surprised that she knew this. "Nothing's changed from what you already know. We've got a lot of problems to deal with."

"What would you say is the biggest problem the endangered fish are facing?"

Tanner didn't hesitate to respond. "That's easy. The hydroelectric dams. They're impregnable for fish to pass through."

Her eyes crinkled as she thought this over. "Unfortunately we can't do anything about that."

"You're right, Ms. Lawton. Saving our endangered fish has proven to be a challenge we're determined to meet."

She smiled politely, speaking in a soft, confident tone. "I don't see why the solutions are complicated. We just tell the farmers, ranchers and loggers what they can and can't do. Then we enforce it, giving the streams and fish time to recover from the abuse. And please, call me Zoë."

Not if he could help it. Instead, he cleared his throat. "The farmers and ranchers only care about their livelihoods, not a bunch of fish that have landed on the endangered-species list."

"That's true," Chuck said. "Two years ago, we had four hundred angry farmers and loggers picketing our building like a pack of sharks. They were furious with the changes we were trying to make because it jeopardized their incomes. Now Tanner and his team have them at least listening to our ideas. But progress has been slow."

Zoë crossed her long legs. Her lovely eyes narrowed, her soft mouth hardening with determination. "We can't afford to make slow progress. Something must be done now. I have instructions to put a stop to the abuses and improve the situation along Bingham River. My boss in

Portland expects nothing less. And that's what I intend to do."

"We're interested in the same thing," Tanner assured her, feeling protective of his efforts with the farmers and loggers. Over the past three years, he'd made a lot of progress in helping the endangered fish. They didn't need this woman's interference. The last thing he wanted was for an outsider to come in and mess up all his hard work.

"That's right," Chuck agreed. "And I think you'll find that Tanner is the one man who has the acumen to deal with all our water users. He has a special touch for getting the ranchers and loggers to cooperate with us in helping improve the spawning runs."

Chuck tossed Tanner a smile full of confidence, but in his eyes, Tanner detected a glint of warning. As the forest supervisor, Chuck didn't want to upset the marine biologist from the National Marine Fisheries Service. Tanner reminded himself they were all working for the good of the endangered fish, but he was also smart enough to know that politics weighed heavily in this equation. Any failure on Tanner's part would trickle downhill. It could make Chuck look bad, which would bounce down onto Tanner's head.

So Tanner must not fail. Even if it meant working with an attractive marine biologist like Zoë Lawton.

"We obviously want the same things. So where do we start?" Zoë asked.

Tanner unrolled a large map and pointed out particularly troublesome areas along the river. The group discussed each issue at length.

"When can we go out to look at some of these sites?" Zoë asked.

Tanner couldn't help being pleasantly surprised. At least she seemed eager and willing. "I've already set up some interviews with a few farmers on Saturday morning."

She hesitated, her forehead creasing with a frown. "Does it have to be on Saturday?"

"That's the best time for the farmers. When we accommodate their schedules, they're more friendly and willing to hear us out." Tanner hoped she wouldn't demand the farmers meet her timetable.

"I can go, but my son will need to tag along. I don't have child care on Saturdays. Is that okay?"

Oh, no. Not the kid. A sinking feeling of dread settled in Tanner's stomach. The last thing he wanted was to spend his weekend with this lovely woman and her talkative little boy.

"That'll be fine," Chuck said.

With his boss sanctioning it, Tanner had little choice but to agree. "We'll leave from here. Meet me in the parking lot at eight a.m. and plan to be gone most of the day."

"Will do." Zoë scooted back her chair and stood gracefully before turning to shake first Gary's, then Ron's hand. When she reached toward Tanner, she met his gaze without flinching. "Thank you for this enlightening discussion. I look forward to working with you."

Tanner pasted a smile on his face, but inside he was screaming. Why did she have to be so friendly and stunning?

As he left the conference room and sauntered down the hall to his office, he couldn't help feeling sabotaged by his boss. Over the next few months, there were a myriad of creeks and streams along the river that he and Zoë would have to traverse. But Tanner didn't have to like it. He could be civil but remote and professional. Above all else, he must protect his work.

Chapter Three

❧

"Jonah, we're late!" Zoë kept her voice calm as she stood at the front door holding her son's jacket.

Though morning sunlight streamed through their living room window, the boy yawned and stumbled down the hallway as if it were the middle of the night. Wearing a pair of blue jeans, a sweatshirt and tennis shoes, he rubbed his sleepy eyes. Zoë handed him his jacket, then bent down to tie his dangling shoelaces. The boy's blond hair still stuck up in back, despite her best efforts with the spray bottle and comb to flatten it down.

"Why do we have to go so early?" He

slipped his little arms into the sleeves of the jacket.

Zoë stood and zipped it up. "I told you already. I have to work, but I thought we could make it a fun outing."

Not much fun getting up early on a Saturday morning.

"But I wanna watch cartoons."

"We may see some fish and I made us a picnic lunch." She lifted her brows, trying to coax a smile out of him.

He didn't disappoint her. His startling blue eyes widened. "Great! Are we going fishing, too?"

She shook her head. "Not today, but soon."

To make their day a bit more fun for Jonah, she'd tucked a canister of homemade chocolate-chip cookies into their lunchbox for dessert.

"Where we going?" His fingers tightened around hers as they walked out to the car.

"I'm not sure. You remember the man

whose truck you hit with the shopping cart?"

"Yeah. He didn't like us much." He gave her a dubious frown.

"His name is Tanner Bohlman and it turns out he's the man I'll be working with this summer."

"Uh-oh." Jonah's eyes widened with worry.

"Don't fret about scratching his truck anymore. It's been dealt with," she insisted.

He gave her a trusting smile and she couldn't resist kissing his forehead.

She opened the car door and he hopped inside before she helped him with his seat belt. She then pressed a bacon, egg and cheese sandwich into his hand for him to eat along the way.

Jonah bit into the sandwich and chewed vigorously. "He's with the Forest Service?"

"Yes, and he wants to take us out today to show us some of the irrigation ditches where salmon are getting lost."

She closed his door, then rounded the car and climbed into the driver's seat. As she clicked on her own seat belt, she glanced at Jonah and noticed a crumb of bread clinging to his chin. She gestured toward it and he wiped his mouth. She started the engine and put the car into gear.

"What if he's still sore with me about what happened?" Jonah said.

As they backed out of the driveway and pulled into traffic, Zoë lowered her sun visor and tried to reassure her son. "Don't worry, I think he's gotten over that."

Or had he? Jonah was right. The man didn't seem to like them very much, and she hoped he wouldn't hold a grudge. No matter what, she had a job to do and didn't want anything to get in the way of her work.

When they pulled into the parking lot of the supervisor's office thirteen minutes later, Tanner stood outside, wearing the spruce-green pants and drab olive-green shirt of a forest ranger. His bronze shield gleamed in the morning sunshine. Since it was Saturday, she was surprised to see him wearing his uniform. She'd expected casual attire like she was wearing. But then she thought better of it. They were on official business today and Tanner looked the part.

Leaning against his truck, he folded his arms and crossed his ankles. A deep frown marred his high forehead. If not for his gruff manners, he'd be a strikingly handsome man. And she couldn't help wondering what had made him so grouchy.

Barring the door on that thought, Zoë parked her car next to his truck and killed the motor.

Jonah peered out the window as he unbuckled his seat belt. "He don't look too happy, Mom."

"*Doesn't* look happy." She corrected his grammar. "And his mood might have something to do with the fact that we're almost ten minutes late."

"Sorry, Mom."

She got out and opened the back door,

leaning over to press a kiss against Jonah's warm cheek before gazing lovingly into his eyes. "Don't worry about it, sweetheart. We're not in a hurry today. Let's just have fun, okay?"

"Work can be fun?" he asked.

"Absolutely. I have fun working all the time." Which was true. She loved her job. Except for Jonah and the Lord, it was the most important thing in her life.

"Then let's go to work." Jonah returned her smile.

As she drew away, he zipped out of the car so fast she didn't have time to stop him. "Jonah, wait."

Too late. He was gone.

With a deep sigh, she reached for the picnic basket and another bag of towels and dry clothes she'd brought just in case she got wet taking water samples. She locked the car and followed as fast as she could.

Like a stealth bomber, Jonah headed straight toward Tanner. Zoë hurried to follow, unsure of Tanner's mood.

The man unfolded his arms and stepped away from his truck. As Jonah approached, Tanner held his hands up as if to protect himself. A flash of uncertainty filled his eyes, then was gone so fast that Zoë thought she must have imagined it. Maybe Tanner wasn't used to being around little kids. Surely he wasn't afraid of Jonah.

"Hi, Tanner!" Jonah called.

"Mr. Bohlman." Zoë corrected her son's rudeness.

"He can call me Tanner." Tanner's voice sounded low and nervous as his gaze flickered over to Zoë.

"I'm sorry we're late. My little sleepy-head couldn't seem to get up this morning. But I told him you wouldn't mind." She ruffled her son's hair and smiled fondly, hoping her declaration would ease Tanner's tension just a bit.

It didn't work. If anything, his shoulders stiffened more.

Jonah jutted his chin toward the ugly scratches still marring the side of Tanner's truck. "You're not mad at me anymore, are you?"

Oh, the innocent sincerity of a young child.

"No. Forget about it," Tanner said.

Zoë gazed at the man, trying to see the truth in his eyes. His blank expression gave her no clues. She hated playing games and decided to take Tanner at his word. If he said he wasn't bothered by the scratches, then she shouldn't be, either. But she sure wished he'd let her pay for the repairs.

"Shall we go?" she asked.

"Yeah, let me help you with that."

He reached to take the picnic basket and bag from her. His fingertips felt warm and roughened by calluses as they brushed against her hand. He jerked back, as though he'd been burned. She couldn't read his expression as he turned and opened the door of his truck so she and Jonah could climb inside.

"We're not taking a Forest Service vehicle?" she asked as she settled into her seat.

He shook his head, staring at the basket with pensive eyes. "No, it wouldn't look good with Jonah along. Someone might complain that we're using a federal vehicle for personal use."

Her mouth dropped open. "Why would they do that?"

He shrugged his broad shoulders. "Beats me. One of my friends almost got fired over such a trivial thing."

"Because he had one of his children in a government vehicle?"

"Yep. People don't stop to realize the long hours a forest ranger works. Sometimes they take their family with them up into the mountains just so they can spend some time together. Since we'll have Jonah with us today, I figure it's best to take my own vehicle. Better safe than sorry."

She never knew. But then, she figured she had a lot to learn on this new assignment. She'd lived in large cities all her life, spending the majority of her time in a lab. She'd never worked out in the field with farmers, ranchers, or logging and mining operations. As long as she helped resolve some of the fishery problems, the inconvenience of moving to this tiny town would be worth it.

"What's this?" He gestured to the basket.

"Our lunch. Since we'll be gone most of the day, I thought we might get hungry."

He frowned. "I didn't think about that."

She laughed, trying to lighten him up with a bit of humor. "You must not have any kids."

"Nope." His jaw hardened as he stashed the basket in the backseat.

Oh, dear. This wasn't working out the way she'd hoped. Was he like this with everyone he met or just her?

She glanced at his ring finger and found it bare. Not even a hint of a shadow. That didn't mean he wasn't in a relationship, but he didn't have the manners of a married man. Maybe he just liked to keep to himself. Or maybe, from the way he kept tossing covert, grumpy looks in her direction, he just didn't like her. She didn't know why that would be, but maybe keeping things between them professional would be best. She didn't want a romantic entanglement right now. She had her hands full with her job and raising her son.

She jerked her thumb toward Jonah. "With this kid always asking for food, I learned to always have snacks on hand. Don't worry. We have plenty for you, too."

He hesitated, a look of open amazement on his face. As if he couldn't believe she'd provide for him, too. Then he rounded the truck and got into the driver's seat before addressing her comment. "You don't need to feed me."

She gave a soft laugh, wishing he wasn't so handsome. "Don't worry. We're happy to share."

"Wait till you taste Mom's cookies." Jonah leaned close to Tanner's side and shielded his mouth with one hand as he whispered loudly, "But she thinks I don't know about them, so act surprised when she gets them out, okay?"

Tanner laughed, a spontaneous sound that rumbled deep in his chest. "I think the cat's out of the bag now."

He indicated Zoë with his chin. Jonah glanced at his mother and realized that she'd overheard every word.

"Ah!" the boy groaned and covered his face with his hands.

She gave him a scolding look. "I take it you did a little peeking this morning while I was getting dressed."

"Just a little," Jonah said.

And yet, she hadn't been able to get him out of bed. She shook her head, never understanding the workings of a child's mind.

Tanner chuckled and Zoë couldn't deny that she found the sound delightful. Finally. Finally they'd broken through his harsh exterior.

"You should do that more often," she said.

"What?" Tanner inserted the key into the ignition and started the engine.

"Laugh."

He flushed a deep red color, looking mortified. Which made her laugh, in turn.

"Don't worry, I won't tell anyone," she said. "We wouldn't want to ruin your fierce reputation."

As if trying to ignore her comments, Tanner glanced at Jonah. "How old are you?"

"Six. I play T-ball. I can hit the ball clearrrr across the field." He opened his little arms wide to make his point. "Next fall, I'll be in second grade. Do you like to fish?"

Tanner blinked, as though trying to keep up with the changes in conversation. "Yeah, I like to fish."

"Can we go fishing today?"

Tanner put the truck into gear and pulled out of the parking lot. Over the top of the boy's head, he met Zoë's gaze. "I'm afraid not. We're going to meet with some farmers today. Do you like to fish?"

Jonah shrugged, gazing over the dashboard and out the windshield. "Don't know. Remember? I already told you I never been before. But I'd sure like to go sometime."

Tanner looked straight ahead as they approached the intersection.

Jonah kept talking. "My dad used to go fishing when he was a kid. Mom told me so. Even though he died, Mom says he loved me like crazy."

Oh, that hurt. Zoë had never heard Jonah speak so freely about his father. It still left her breathless with pain every time she thought about Derek's death in a skiing accident only eleven months after Jonah's birth. Without warning, all their hopes and dreams had been dashed to pieces. And poor Jonah, left without a father. He didn't even remember his daddy, outside of the things she had told him.

Life could be so unfair.

"Is that so?" Tanner's gaze slid over Zoë, as if seeking the truth in her eyes.

"Yeah, but me and Mom get along just fine. Someday, I suppose she'll get married again. But not without my approval.

She told me so." Jonah sat between them, smiling with anticipation.

"My dad died when I was eight and my mom when I was ten," Tanner said.

Zoë hadn't expected him to confide something so personal. Not to them. Her heart went out to him. Being orphaned so young couldn't have been easy.

"Really? You lost *both* your parents?" Jonah peered at Tanner, his mouth hanging open in astonishment.

"Yep, so I didn't have anyone to take me fishing, either."

Zoë absorbed every word like dry sand soaking up rain. How she wished Jonah could have known his daddy. Knowing that Tanner had faced the same loss left her feeling melancholy.

"Then who taught you to fish?" Jonah asked.

"At first, my grandpa taught me," Tanner said. "We'd go fishing and then come home and eat my grandma's homemade apple pie. It's one of my fondest childhood memories. But he died when I was thirteen. Grandma died a year later."

"Who raised you after your grandparents died?" Zoë asked.

"Foster care." His jaw hardened, as though he'd rather not talk about it.

She didn't blame him.

Jonah heaved a little sigh. "I wish I had a grandpa, but me and Mom are all alone, just like you. Except for God. Mom says we're never really alone, as long as we have the Lord with us."

How profound. In that moment, Zoë realized that all their discussions, all the bedtime prayers and taking her son to Sunday school classes, had actually paid off. In spite of his wiggling and talking during lessons, part of what Jonah had been taught had actually sunk in.

Tanner frowned and turned away, making a pretense of adjusting his rearview mirror. "Some people just use God as a crutch."

"What do you mean by that?" Zoë couldn't help asking.

"Never mind. It's not really an appropriate business topic anyway."

Zoë hesitated to push. It wasn't her business, after all. She worked in a scientific field and had met her share of religious skeptics before, but something in Tanner's eyes told her he'd believed in God once but had somehow lost his faith. "It's Saturday, we're not in the office, we're in your personal truck, so go ahead and talk. I don't mind. Don't you believe in God?"

"Occasionally." He didn't meet her eyes.

"What does that mean?" How could you occasionally believe in the Lord?

"God and I leave each other alone for the most part. It works better for us that way."

She'd never heard such a cynical statement in all her life. She opened her mouth several times, a myriad of comebacks stinging her tongue. But then she remembered that she barely knew this man and had no right to judge him.

"You sound hurt," she said.

"Uh-huh." The firm set of his mouth told her he would say no more.

"Maybe we can go fishing *after* work," Jonah said, seemingly oblivious to their discussion on Deity.

"We're not going fishing today," Zoë said.

"Then when can we go?" he persisted.

"We'll talk about it later." Zoë thought Jonah had said enough for one day.

"Is he always like this?" Tanner asked as they headed out of town.

She decided not to be offended by the question. From Tanner's earnest expression, she didn't believe he meant it as a criticism. "Yes, but he's also an excellent student and gets along with everyone at school."

"Except Brian. He bosses me around all the time. I don't like him much." Jonah made an ugly face.

Tanner chuckled and Zoë thought perhaps she'd misjudged the man. Maybe he wasn't such a hard case after all.

Tanner's fingers tightened around the steering wheel and he took a deep breath, as if he were about to submerge his head underwater. "Tell you what. I like to go fishing, too. How about I take you to Kids' Creek Park in town? They have rainbow trout there and we just seeded the pond with hatchery-raised steelhead salmon. Since it's illegal to catch steelhead in the wild, that's a real treat. I'm sure we could catch your limit."

"That'd be great." Jonah bounced happily on the seat, then paused and quirked one brow. "But what does *seeded* mean?"

Tanner jerked his head toward Zoë. "Ask your mom."

The boy promptly faced his mother and repeated his question.

She smiled and brushed a jagged thatch of blond hair away from his eyes. "It means they brought in a big truck from the fish hatchery filled with smaller steelhead fish and dumped them into the pond, just so kids like you can have fun catching them."

"Except our steelhead aren't small. Most of them are over twelve inches long," Tanner said.

"Wow! Can we go, Mom? Can we?" Jonah wriggled with expectation.

She hesitated. Tanner's invitation had come as a complete surprise. She sensed a subtle tensing in his shoulders and wondered if he regretted his offer. An outing of this sort was just what Jonah needed. She couldn't think of one legitimate reason to say no. "Of course we can go."

"Hooray!" Jonah swiveled around to face Tanner, his little body squirming in anticipation. "When? When can we go?"

"How about tomorrow afternoon?" Tanner smiled but stared straight ahead, keeping his eyes on the road.

"I'm afraid tomorrow is Sunday and I take Jonah to church. What about another day?" Zoë ignored Jonah's irritated gasp. She was eager to worship God and meet their new congregation to make some friends. Then she could trade babysitting on the weekends and set up playdates for Jonah throughout the summer months.

Tanner swiped a hand across the light

stubble on his chin. "I can't go again until next Saturday."

"That would work for us," she agreed.

"But that's a whole week away," Jonah whined.

Zoë squeezed his arm gently to settle him down. "Then that'll give you something fun to look forward to."

"Ah," he grumbled but didn't argue further.

"Where are we going first?" Zoë asked Tanner, hoping to change the subject.

"Out to Harry Ragsdale's farm."

"It's sure beautiful here." Zoë gazed at Bingham River running parallel to the road, taking in the pristine view of clean, rushing water, willows and cottonwoods. Farther out, wide meadows covered with sedges and wire grass added a variety of vibrant green hues.

Tanner nodded in agreement, his expression showing pride in the area where he worked. Somehow sharing this appreciation with him gave them something in common.

They passed a sign that read Ragsdale Farms.

With their focus back on work, the frown returned to Tanner's face. Just when Zoë thought they were making headway and becoming friends, Tanner had to go and disappoint her. She'd just have to remember not to expect anything from him—then she wouldn't be disappointed again.

Chapter Four

The black asphalt gave way to dirt road. The tires of the truck kicked up gravel. Tanner slowed their speed and put on the blinker before turning onto Challis Road.

He must be crazy. What had he been thinking to invite Jonah on a fishing trip? He didn't know a thing about kids. No doubt Zoë would come along. Which meant Tanner would have to be near her in a personal setting as well as at work.

No, he shouldn't have made the offer. But remembering the fun he'd had with Grandpa had made him want the same for Jonah. He didn't even like kids. Or at least he didn't think he did. He'd wanted them once. Oodles of them. But his broken engagement had ended all that. Children were okay for other people, but not for him.

"There's good riffle along the river here," Zoë observed.

Tanner nodded and gazed at the frothing water dashing over the jagged rocks. Riffle oxygenated the spawning beds.

Zoë shielded her eyes against the bright sunlight pouring through the windshield. "How much of the water here is diverted for irrigation?"

Tanner couldn't remember ever meeting a woman who was actually interested in his work. Zoë was quite refreshing. "All but 7 percent. This is a heavy agricultural area and they use almost all the water in the river."

She gave a low whistle. "No wonder there isn't enough for the fish to swim up the lower seven miles of the river."

"We haven't come up with an idea on how to combat that problem yet."

"Do the farmers need to use all the water they take out for irrigation?"

He shrugged. "Probably not, but until we install farmer's screens in all the irrigation ditches, there's no system in place to control their outtake. Maybe you can think of something for us to do until we get all the screens in place."

He'd kiss her if she came up with a solution. This one problem had become a real quandary for them. So far, nothing they'd tried had worked. He doubted that an outsider would be able to think of a solution.

Zoë pointed to an area along the riverbanks with no overhanging willows. "Have you had cattle grazing over there? The riverbanks are caved in and raw. No vegetation growing, which means no redds."

Redds were spawning beds for fish. The eggs needed cold, clean, well-oxygenated water to survive. Without shade from overhanging willows and other vegetation, the temperature of the stream increased and killed off the eggs.

"Yes, the cows have tromped in the stream and broken down the banks here. We convinced several local ranchers to let us fence off parts of the streams to stop this from happening. The area should recover over time."

Gazing out the window, he decided by midweek he could find a valid excuse to call Zoë and cancel the fishing trip with Jonah. There wasn't enough time in his busy schedule to spend fishing with a cute little boy who talked too much anyway. Tanner had been foolish to make the offer.

No, he couldn't do that. His guilty conscience nipped at him. Canceling would break Jonah's heart. And Tanner wasn't that cruel. Not yet anyway.

A kid like Jonah might be a lot of fun. And a lot of hard work, too. Tanner was gaining a new appreciation for Zoë. From his experience with his own mother, he knew that being a single mom wasn't easy, yet Zoë seemed to do it with such calm grace.

He heaved a disgruntled sigh. Tanner

hated the thought of hurting Jonah and losing the boy's trust, though he didn't know why. What Jonah Lawton thought shouldn't matter to Tanner. The boy wasn't his son. They had no connection except that Tanner now worked with Zoë. In spite of trying not to, Tanner still liked the kid.

Too much.

Maybe it was because Tanner understood the hurt of losing his father so young. Then, his mother had been busy working just to put food on the table. No quality time. No one to attend his ball games or help with his science projects. No one to confide his troubles and victories to.

Tanner shook his head, keeping his gaze on the narrow dirt road. They skirted fields of alfalfa, barley and potatoes, the outlying mountains providing a stunning backdrop for meadows and streams twining through the valley. Lovely and serene. Tanner frequently went to the mountains whenever he felt sad or lonely, which was often these days. Out here, he never felt lost or alone.

Until now. Until he'd met Zoë Lawton and her inquisitive little son. He wasn't alone just now, but he still felt lost.

In a matter of days since he'd met them in Harper's Grocery Store parking lot, something had changed for Tanner. Something he couldn't explain. The fact that he didn't know what it was left him feeling disconnected and troubled.

Yep, he'd have to go fishing with Jonah. He couldn't retract the offer. Not without upsetting the boy, and his mother.

The mother.

He tossed a quick glance at Zoë, taking in her faded blue jeans, warm sweater and practical boots. Gone were the professional jacket, skirt and heels that'd almost made him salivate. With her slender legs crossed and her delicate hands resting in her lap, she looked too young to be a professional woman supporting a child.

And a widow.

From what Jonah had said, she'd lost

her husband years ago. Tanner couldn't help wondering if she'd loved the man. If his death had crushed her heart the way Cheryl had crushed his.

As the wheels thumped across the washboard road, he cast surreptitious glances Zoë's way. Her head bobbed gently with the swaying of the vehicle. She looked completely at home, not at all a prissy city girl who couldn't handle a bit of dirt on her clothes. Her smudged eyeliner made her blue eyes appear smoky and mysterious. No matter what this woman wore, she was beautiful.

As they passed the canal, Tanner slowed the truck and pointed at the trench filled with water. "You can see there's no farmer's screen on this irrigation ditch. Last spring, hundreds of fish took the wrong turn in the canal, got lost and ended up in the ditch instead of moving on their way through the river."

Jonah sat up straighter to see out the window. "What happened to them?"

Surprised to find the child listening,

Tanner explained, "With nowhere else to go, they ended up in the fields, dead."

The boy blinked at that. "Dead?"

"Don't worry, sweetheart, we'll do something to stop it from happening again." Zoë patted Jonah's arm.

Tanner didn't think she should promise something she might not be able to deliver. But her confidence made him feel as though they really could resolve the problems they faced.

They rounded the bend and saw a rusty old truck parked at the side of the road. A man in his mid-forties stood near the ditch bank, wearing a baseball cap, blue overalls and knee-high waders. He waved, then propped his shovel in the dirt before leaning his forearms against the top of the handle.

"That's Harry Ragsdale." Tanner pulled over, then killed the motor.

They all got out and joined Harry before Tanner made the introductions.

"I must admit I was a bit surprised when Tanner called to see if I'd meet with you today. What can I do for you?" Harry's ruddy cheeks wobbled slightly as he shook Zoë's hand.

"It's not what you can do for us, but what we can do for you." Zoë spoke right up, her voice pleasant enough. "We need to put a farmer's irrigation screen on your property as soon as possible. We'd like your permission to start work immediately."

Harry shrugged, his doubtful gaze resting heavily on Tanner. "I already told the ranger I can't do that. Screens are a big pain to maintain. They catch garbage and clog up. They have to be constantly cleaned. I don't have time for that kind of nonsense."

Zoë's spine stiffened, her smile fading to a disapproving frown. This didn't look good.

"We have to do something, Mr. Ragsdale. The Endangered Species Act requires it by law," she said.

Harry lifted a hand, as if to shoo away a

fly. "Then do something else. But I'm not gonna put any screens on my property."

Zoë tilted her head and her eyes hardened just a bit. "A screen will keep wayward salmon from swimming past the canal and ending up dead in your ditch."

"I don't care if they do. They rot and provide good fertilizer for my fields."

Zoë's mouth tightened. "But so many fish are dying that they've ended up on the endangered-species list. If you won't maintain a screen, we'll have to get an injunction against you to shut off your water."

"What?" The word exploded from Harry's mouth like a nuclear detonation. "You can't do that. I need water for my crops. Shutting off my water would put me out of business."

"You're leaving us no other choice," Zoë insisted.

Tanner held up both hands. This wasn't what he'd expected at all. "Now, now, that won't be necessary. We can deal with this situation without resorting to shutting off your water."

Zoë glared at Tanner as if he'd just slapped her face. "Then, what do you recommend?"

"I can't afford to install a farmer's screen." Harry's voice vibrated with anger. "All that cement and steel. It'd cost me thousands of dollars."

Jonah stepped closer to his mother, sliding his hand into hers as his eyes creased with worry over their raised voices. A protective impulse swarmed Tanner's chest and he longed to comfort the child. Maybe he shouldn't have agreed to bring the kid along. From the way Zoë patted the boy's cheek in a reassuring gesture, she was having second thoughts, too.

"You won't have to pay a dime of the costs, Harry. FRIMA has given us a grant to fund the project. We just need your permission to have it installed. We'll do all the work." Placing one hand on the other man's shoulder, Tanner looked into his eyes, a tactic he frequently used to calm irate farmers.

"What's FRIMA?" Harry asked in a gruff voice.

"The Fisheries Restoration and Irrigation Mitigation Act. They're a voluntary, nonregulatory program that provides funding to screen water diversions. All you need to do is help ensure that it's maintained. Can you do that if it means keeping the fish out of your ditches and moving in a safe passageway?"

"Well, um, yes, I suppose if you're gonna pay for it, I can at least help maintain it," Harry said.

"Good! I knew we could count on your help." Tanner smiled, hoping to lighten the tense mood.

Zoë's face flooded with color and Tanner could tell she was upset. Didn't she realize that angering the local farmers would never help them achieve their goals? Threats would just get everyone fighting mad.

Harry smiled and nodded at Tanner but

tossed a sneer at Zoë. And that's when Tanner realized that she'd just made an enemy who would talk to the other farmers in the area. Word would soon spread like wildfire that they had a hard-nosed federal marine biologist in town. Tanner knew how it worked. He'd been at this game a long time now.

Tanner needed to talk to Zoë in private. He should have explained things better before he brought her out here. Letting her face an irate farmer hadn't been Tanner's intent, but he'd had no idea when Harry resisted their proposal that she'd make such a do-or-die threat.

"Okay, I'll set it up and be in touch with you soon," Tanner told Harry.

"Good, you do that. You can call me anytime," Harry said.

As they walked back to Tanner's truck, Zoë didn't say a word. From her narrowed eyes, he realized this wasn't over. She was very upset. At him. He could almost imagine hot steam jetting from her ears, eyes and nose. He figured she was keeping her silence because of Jonah. But once they were alone again, he dreaded the inevitable flare-up that was sure to follow.

Zoë bit down on the inside of her cheek to keep from telling Tanner what she really thought about the way he'd coddled Harry Ragsdale. No doubt he was doing the same kind of appeasement with the other farmers in the area. And what about the ranchers and logging companies?

Glancing at Jonah, she almost wished she hadn't brought her son along. She was angry and burned to give Tanner a piece of her mind. But she didn't want to have harsh words with Tanner in front of her little boy. For now, she clamped her mouth closed and thought of calm, professional words she should say to Tanner later on.

Tanner drove them out to meet with two more farmers, with the same results as the first. One farmer argued, even when Tanner told him that FRIMA would cover the expense. The farmer didn't want the nuisance of dealing with a screen. He didn't want to be bothered.

And then Zoë stepped in with her usual blunt candor, which triggered Tanner into cajoling the man to get him to agree. The way Tanner tried to accommodate each farmer made Zoë think Tanner was part of the problem rather than the solution. No wonder so many fish were dying!

By the time noon rolled around and Tanner parked his truck near a campground at the base of the Bingham Mountains, Zoë seethed with annoyance. She didn't want to be so hard-nosed, but she had her orders. Her employment was riding on her success here. With a young son to raise, she couldn't afford to lose her job.

While Jonah raced ahead to play by the stream that threaded its way through the tall cottonwoods, Zoë reached for her bag and their lunch. She then walked with Tanner toward a picnic table nearby.

"Jonah, don't go too far. Stay where I can see you," she called as the boy bent over the shallow creek and poked the water with a stick.

Tanner tugged the picnic basket from her hand and carried it for her. Finally they were alone and she could have a private word with him. Taking a deep breath, she vowed to remain civil.

"Who do you think you are?" she asked quietly.

Okay, that didn't come out the way she'd intended. She was so troubled that her emotions seemed to burst out of her mouth.

His response sounded just as clipped, telling her that he was also flustered by today's events. "I'm the Fisheries and Wildlife staff officer over this national forest. We want to get these people's attention, but we also need their cooperation. And we can't do that with threats. If we're gonna solve these problems, we need the support of the farmers."

Zoë wasn't so sure that was true. And yet, she didn't want to cause more problems, either. She felt like an astronaut in outer space, not quite sure of herself anymore. "They've already taken too much advantage, Tanner. These problems didn't happen overnight. They happened over years and years of abuse. The fish are out of time. Coaxing and being nice will take too long. We need action right now."

"And you think threats will work better?"

"When people refuse to do what's right, yes. We have the law on our side."

His dark eyes met hers. "Threats only work as a last resort," he said. "But I've found that we can get a lot of cooperation from these people if we show them what the problem is and offer to help them solve it. If we fix problems by cramming solutions down their throats, we just end up with a bunch of congressional inquiries."

She tilted her head in confusion, never quite taking her eyes off Jonah. "Congressional inquiries?"

He nodded. "That's right. The farmers and ranchers have a direct line to their senators, whom they support with reelection funds. And believe me, their senators listen to *everything* they have to say."

He chuckled without humor and she realized he was serious.

"But congressional inquiries?" she said again. "They really resort to such drastic measures?"

He hitched one shoulder. "Would you really resort to shutting off their water?"

She nibbled at the end of her pinkie finger, thinking this over. "Yes, I would."

"Well, so would they. Before I came here, we had congressional inquiries all the time. The Steelhead National Forest doesn't need politicians breathing down our necks. Which is what will happen if Harry Ragsdale and other farmers like him start making angry phone calls."

No, that wouldn't be good. It'd stir up a pot they didn't want stirred and delay getting the job done even longer. Zoë never knew working at the local level could be so complicated.

"I can certainly understand why you want to avoid that," she agreed.

But what about her orders? Her boss in Portland had made it very clear what he expected her to accomplish this summer. There wasn't any room for pampering.

"So you can see why I tried to be pleasant with Harry Ragsdale instead of bullying him," Tanner said.

"Did I bully him?" The thought made her feel horrible. She didn't want to bully anyone. She was just trying to do her job.

His handsome mouth flashed with a brief smile, telling her that she'd surprised him today. "Yes, and you're the prettiest bully I've come across lately."

His words caught her off guard and her cheeks flushed with heat. From the sudden color in his face and the way he quickly looked away, she could tell he'd let the compliment slip out without thinking.

Okay, better to forget about his flattering remark. She'd just let it drop.

"I'm sorry I didn't warn you before we came out here. I should have explained the situation to you better," he said.

She appreciated his apology, but it didn't

solve anything right now. "Then what do you propose? If farmers won't agree to let us install the screens on their property, then we'll need to force them to comply."

He snorted. "Good luck with that tactic."

Zoë couldn't help feeling bitter about the situation. From what she'd seen, most people didn't care. They just wanted to go on with their lives, without any inconvenience to themselves. And Tanner seemed to be letting them do it. "I just don't like the way you baby them."

"I'm not babying them. I'm working to get results we can all live with." He set the basket on the picnic table.

Biting her tongue, Zoë spread out a thin cloth, then unpacked their lunch. She kept her face toward the stream, watching Jonah.

Tanner stood at the edge of the table, hands in his pockets. Zoë quashed the urge to apologize. Not when she really believed he was wrong in his tactics. And frankly, she had the power to override him. She didn't want to do that and cause more friction between them, but she'd do it if she had to.

"At least we got them each to agree to the screens," he said lamely.

She handed him a paper plate with a turkey-and-Swiss-cheese sandwich and a handful of grapes and rippled potato chips on the side. "Three down and zillions more to go."

His frosty gaze brushed past hers in a dismissive glance. "We'll deal with each of them."

"Hey, I saw little fish swimming in the stream," Jonah gasped as he joined them. "But they don't have any fins. Just a long tail."

He plopped down on the bench and snatched up a sandwich, seemingly oblivious to the dark stares from the adults nearby.

"That's nice, sweetheart. But I'll bet they're tadpoles, not fish," Zoë said.

"Tadpoles?" Jonah's brow crinkled as he took a bite and chewed.

"Baby frogs. You saw them once in Portland, remember? And we need to bless the food before we eat it." She answered patiently, surprised at her serene voice when she was feeling anything but calm inside. Why could she maintain her composure with Jonah but not with Tanner?

Conscious of Tanner's troubled frown resting on her, she offered a quick prayer. She and Tanner ate their lunches in silence, listening to Jonah's happy chatter. She answered the child's melee of questions about tadpoles with quick, succinct sentences. Only when Zoë brought out the cookies did Tanner speak to her again.

"These are delicious. They taste just like the ones my grandma used to make. Soft and chocolaty." He held up his fourth cookie, a big bite taken out of the side as he chewed with relish.

"Thank you." At least she'd done something right today. But she didn't like the tension between them. She didn't like feeling like an ogre.

Later, Zoë packed everything up while Tanner went to the creek with Jonah. At one point, she looked up and saw Tanner holding her son's hand, assisting the boy so he could cross the water without falling in. Seeing this man helping her little son reminded her that Derek was gone and wouldn't be coming back.

Thinking about her husband caused her throat to ache, as though an icy fist squeezed it tight. How she longed for the companionship and intimacy she'd shared with her husband. Someone to talk to who really cared.

Someone who loved her as much as she loved him.

Shaking off her black mood, she returned the basket to the truck and got out her hip waders and sample kit. At the side of Clear Creek, she pulled on the green rubber waders. Then she opened her kit and took out several empty, tubelike glass vials. She dipped some into the water and some into the muddy bank for soil samples. As she pressed the cap onto the last vial and labeled the little jar, she became aware of Tanner standing nearby with Jonah.

"You taking some samples?" Tanner said.

"Yep." She slipped the vial into her pocket before reaching for her fishnet. Holding still as the water swirled around her knees, she waited until a trout swam by. With quick movements, she scooped up the fish with the net. Keeping the thrashing animal in the water, she leaned down and gently clasped it with her hands, turning it upside down so its gleaming white belly faced her. The fish immediately quieted as she inspected it with her hands.

"Rainbow trout?" Tanner asked.

"Yes, eight inches long and in good health." She didn't look up as she measured the fish against the notches carved in the handle of the net.

She let the fish go and it zipped away while she pulled out a small notebook and jotted down the information.

"You've obviously handled a lot of fish, yet you've never gone fishing."

"That's right." She didn't offer an explanation. She hadn't thought about it until now, but she never seemed to have enough extra time for leisure activities. Until recently. Although their scheduled fishing trip was mostly about Jonah, she also looked forward to the experience. But she didn't want to tell Tanner that. He might get the wrong idea.

"Okay, that's it. I'm done for now." She stowed her notebook in the pocket of her shirt, then reached for a boulder to grasp so she could pull herself out of the stream. She found Tanner's hand in front of her, his long fingers extended. Surprised by his offering, she gazed up at his stony face for several moments. As he pulled her up, she felt his great physical strength. She didn't look at him as she rinsed the mud from her waders, dried them off, then folded them to carry back to the truck.

Jonah sped ahead of them, hopping over clumps of grass, kicking at a rock and laughing. Having a great time.

"I appreciate your getting those samples." Tanner spoke beside her.

An unexplainable irritation gnawed at her gut. "It's my job."

"I know. But I didn't even think about it, until I saw you doing it."

She faced him. "And why is that so surprising, Tanner?"

"I, um… It's not." His face flushed with embarrassment, his hands in his pockets like a little kid who'd just been caught stealing a pack of gum.

"It's your strategy in dealing with the farmers I don't agree with," he said.

"Is that right?" She bit back a harsher response.

His shoulders relaxed somewhat and his gaze softened. "Look, I didn't mean to offend you, Zoë. I don't know many women who would tromp through a stream to gather mud samples," he said.

His confession left her speechless for several moments. "We definitely have different methods. I'd like to take these samples to my office now, if you don't mind."

Turning, she kept walking, conscious of him following behind. Back in the truck, they didn't speak much as Tanner drove them down the mountain and back to town. In the supervisor's parking lot, Zoë gathered her bags and moved them over to her car.

Before she took Jonah home, the boy looked up at Tanner with a charming smile. "Don't forget our fishing trip next Saturday."

"I won't." Tanner spoke low.

Zoë opened her mouth to tell Tanner that she'd changed her mind about them going, but she couldn't stand to hurt her son that way. It wasn't Jonah's fault that she was having an altercation with Tanner over their methods.

Tanner took a deep inhale of resignation. "I'll pick you up at nine."

"Do you know where we live?" she asked.

"I do. It's a small town."

Right. She got it. But she still didn't know if they should go.

"Thanks for taking us out today." She said the words mechanically.

"You're welcome. I've got another trip planned for us midweek, to visit one of the logging operations. I'll call your office on Monday to give you the exact time. I'll pick you up at your office."

Yeah, that would be fun. She couldn't wait.

She nodded, her gaze glancing off his. "Fine, I'll let my assistant know."

And without another word, they parted company on that sour note.

Chapter Five

Midweek came much too soon for Tanner's peace of mind. With Zoë in the passenger seat, he drove a Forest Service truck this time as they headed up the mountain. For some crazy reason, Tanner missed the incessant chatter of her son. Against his better judgment, Tanner had come to like the boy. He tried to tell himself the kid was just another coworker's little boy, but for some reason Tanner felt different about Jonah.

"How's Jonah?" he couldn't help asking Zoë.

"Great. He can't wait for our fishing trip on Saturday."

"Good." Tanner figured if he had to go, the least he could do was make it fun for Jonah.

Part of him wondered if he was setting himself up for more pain by letting himself care for Jonah.

But really it wasn't that big a deal. Taking the kid fishing didn't mean they had to be best buddies forever. It wouldn't hurt to be nice to a fatherless child.

Or would it?

As before, the road leading toward the mountains paralleled Bingham River. Willows, sedges and grass edged the riverbanks, the frothing stream splashing over smoothed boulders in its path. The water glimmered in the sunlight, like a million translucent crystals.

"It's so pretty up here," Zoë said, awestruck. "I just can't get over how beautiful this river is."

Tanner nodded in silent agreement, enjoying the moment. Glad to share it with someone who appreciated nature as much as he did. If only they didn't conflict on their approach to work, everything would be fine.

"Where are we going today?" she asked.

"There's a logging operation working up by Silver Peak. The Western Logging Company. I need to check on their work cleanup and thought you'd find it interesting."

She glanced at him, her delicate brows pulled down in a doubtful expression. Maybe he sounded a bit brusque, though he didn't mean to. He felt too comfortable around this woman. He didn't understand why he seemed to open up and say things to Zoë that he normally would have bit his tongue on. And the realization that he liked her made him tense up like a tightly wound top.

"You okay?" she asked.

No! I don't want you or your little boy getting me to open up.

"Sure, I'm fine."

She settled back in her seat, her movements causing her delicate fragrance to waft through the air. He turned his head away, but not before he'd breathed in deeply.

He didn't know what he thought anymore, and his insides knotted in frustration. But he knew she made him feel again, and that was dangerous.

Their trip up the dirt road took an hour as they climbed in elevation. Tall lodgepole pine, spruce and fir flowed across the Bingham Mountains in a carpet of green.

"This cutblock shows recent activity." Zoë pointed to where trees had been freshly cut.

The cutblock was an area where timber had been sold to the logging operation to be harvested and cut out. Then the Forest Service would come in later and replant.

"Yes, this is where I want to check their cleanup. We've had a few infractions with this company before, but nothing serious."

Zoë scanned the area, her expression darkening. "Can you pull over, please?"

He stopped the truck, wondering what she'd seen to upset her. Deciding to be patient, he followed her lead. If nothing else, he wanted to see how well she knew her business.

Without waiting for him, she climbed out and headed toward the boundary of the cutblock. Then she wandered into the buffer zone around the public road and the stream where trees were not to be cut. Hopping over rocks and tree stumps in her path, she headed toward the creek that meandered down below. Tanner had to hustle to keep up with her brisk stride. He'd been foolish to ever think this woman was too feminine to get involved with the work here. The uneven ground didn't hinder her booted feet in the least.

Now and then, she paused beside piles of slash left behind by the timber operation: cut tree limbs, stumps and tops lying forgotten on the ground, their drying leaves and nettles turning brittle and brown.

"This is what you call cleanup?" Resting a hand on her hip, Zoë stared at the debris and murmured the words as if to herself.

"No, it isn't, but they may have accidentally missed this slash," Tanner said, though he was none too happy with the poor job the timber operation had done cleaning up this area.

She pointed at more slash as she walked among the trees. "By next spring, every bit of this trash will have washed down into Tilting Creek and blocked the stream. And the silt from erosion will suffocate the redds. No fish will thrive here. This has got to be cleared out. Right now."

She didn't raise her voice, but there was no mistaking her resolve. He agreed with her deductions.

"You take your work very seriously." Without thinking, he reached out and wiped a dark splotch of dirt off her chin. When he realized what he'd done, he jerked back.

She kept walking, barely sparing him a glance.

Though he admired her ferocity on behalf of the fish, he also feared that she might create unneeded animosity with the Western Logging Company. But how could he stop it?

"They'll clean it up, all right," he assured her. "It's in their contract. I'll take care of it. A quick reminder, and they'll get the slash out of here within a few days."

"I hope so." She turned and headed toward the water, not yet finished with her tour.

Following the skidding trail, she hurried past the empty area once populated by Douglas fir, larch and cedar. The sour scent of sawdust filled Tanner's nose.

When she reached the creek, Zoë stopped, her body as rigid as a brick wall. Tanner caught up with her and lifted his head. His jaw dropped open in surprise and a flush of anger caused his skin to burn. Great mounds of soil had been pushed into the creek to allow bulldozers to cross the stream. The skidding tracks of large machinery could still be seen in the mud, cutting across the pool of water blocked by the torn-up earth. Had the skidder accidentally caved in the bank as it had turned around? Or had this been done on purpose?

Only a slim column of water was able to slide past. The vegetation and the stream would die if something wasn't done to rectify this problem fast.

Zoë looked at Tanner, her blue eyes as cold as chipped ice as she gestured toward the muddy pool. "They've dammed up this creek. No wonder the fish can't get through to spawn."

Tanner raked a hand through his short hair, beyond frustrated. "Yeah, they sure have."

"What are you going to do about it?" she asked in a quiet voice.

Her question worried him, but he wanted to keep a cool head. "I'm gonna demand they fix it, and possibly levy a fine. Let's go have a chat with them."

No way was he going to let the timber operation get away with this violation. If Zoë hadn't stopped him and gotten out of the truck to take a closer look, he would have missed this…until the problem got much worse. At this point, they could repair the damage without lasting consequences. If he hadn't discovered it now, the harm would have taken years to repair.

She accompanied him back to the truck, moving just as fast as when they'd come downhill. He could barely keep up with her pace. Again, he couldn't believe he ever thought her too feminine for her profession.

"I'll let you do most of the talking, okay?" she offered.

"Thanks." Tanner blew out a breath of relief. She was understandably upset, just like him. And yet, she deferred to him. She was learning fast.

Back in the truck, they didn't speak as they approached the landing area of the timber operation. Tanner's body tensed with irritation as he thought about what he should say to the logging boss.

The buzz of engines filled the air. Tanner parked the Forest Service truck over by the boss's trailer office. As he got out and headed for the small structure with Zoë close beside him, the cacophony of heavy equipment and chain saws almost deafened him.

Zoë stood outside while Tanner went inside the trailer to look for the foreman. No one there. He walked toward the deck area, conscious of the loud noise and potential danger moving around him. Zoë stayed right beside him all the way, her long legs matching his stride for stride.

Several double logging trucks with four eight-foot bunks in each bed sat off to one side, waiting to be filled with timber. Piles of felled tree trunks sat nearby. A crane moved rapidly overhead, its spindly hooks whisking two eighty-foot logs through the air before laying them neatly in the hayracks of the trucks.

A crawler tractor the size of a small house moved with burdensome stealth across the deck, its steel treads cleating into the ground to give it the traction and power to push or pull heavy loads. A bulldozer the same size sat silent to one side, its front blade mottled with clumps of grass and damp earth. Rubber-tired skidders, equipped with heavy chains and chokers, pulled long trunks of trees over to the landing area.

Suffocating dust filled the air, and both Tanner and Zoë put a hand over their noses to protect their lungs.

"Where's the wood boss?" Tanner yelled at a deckhand wearing an orange vest and hard hat.

The young man turned and wiped a gloved hand across his blackened face. He didn't bother speaking over the roar of noise but pointed toward the skidder, which had paused to idle while the operator shouted down at another man wearing a bright red hard hat and holding a clipboard.

As they approached, the operator pointed at them, winning the attention of the wood boss. The man turned to see them, his gaze lowering briefly to the federal shield Tanner wore on the front of his uniform shirt. A brief blaze of panic flashed in the man's eyes, then was gone. And that's when Tanner knew the truth. Though the wood boss

constantly made excuses, he'd intentionally allowed his crew to violate their contract. And because of Zoë, they'd caught
him at it.

Zoë inhaled a shallow breath, trying not
to breathe in any more dust than necessary. Tanner touched her arm, making her
aware of a forklift coming up on her right
side. It did no good to talk in this environment. No one could hear over the roar
of machinery, but she saw the danger and
moved away.

The wood boss jutted his chin and
pointed toward the trailer office. Tanner
stepped back, letting Zoë go in front of
him as they followed the man and stepped
inside the cramped trailer. Tanner shut
the door, immediately cutting off enough
noise that Zoë could hear herself think.

"Dale, this is Zoë Lawton, the new marine biologist with the National Marine
Fisheries Service." Tanner smiled amiably
as he made the introductions.

"Glad to meet you, Ms. Lawton." Dale

reached forward and shook her hand, which she held out like a brick of cement. She didn't smile, but she gave the man a curt nod of recognition.

"Dale, I think you know why I'm here," Tanner said.

"No, I didn't expect to see you today. What's up?" He removed his hard hat, revealing shaggy, sweat-dampened hair. He scratched his chin, his short nails rasping across the gray stubble.

"You've left slash all over the buffer zone." Tanner jerked a thumb toward the direction from which they'd come.

"We did?" Dale's voice sounded innocent and a tad wheedling.

Zoë wasn't fooled but resigned herself to letting Tanner handle this. She was learning to let him do his job and only interfere as a last resort.

"We must have missed it. I'm sure it was just an accidental oversight," Dale said.

Not likely. Not from the nervous way the man was acting.

"You've got one week to clean it up."

"We can do that, no problem," Dale agreed, his head bobbing like a panicked rooster.

"Good. And one more thing." Tanner paused, his gaze locked with Dale's…a difficult thing to do since the man was trying to look everywhere but at Tanner. "You've dammed up Tilting Creek."

Dale's jaw dropped, his eyes wide with shock. "No! Really? I didn't know."

Zoë forced back a snort. Oh, this was a good act.

Tanner shot her a warning look and she bit her tongue. "Yes, really. And you'll have it cleaned up by this afternoon."

The wood boss looked stunned. "This afternoon? We can't get it done that fast. I've got my men assigned to other jobs today. I'd have to pull them off their work. It'd take at least two days to move the heavy machines back down by the creek to clean it out."

"Then you'd better get to it," Tanner said.

"Oh, we'll get it cleaned up all right,

but I'll need a couple of weeks at least. I mean, be realistic." Dale gave them a cajoling smile, his sun-wrinkled eyes showing lines of dirt streaking out toward his temples.

Something hardened inside Zoë. There was nothing she hated more than brussels sprouts, cruelty to children and liars. As her gaze met Tanner's, she saw his eyes smolder with anger. Good! She was glad to see he was also offended by this situation. Though his voice sounded calm and logical, his words sliced through any doubts she might have had about him.

"You can't have that long, Dale. You'll get it cleaned up before I drive back out here tomorrow afternoon to check your work. Got it?"

"Now, be reasonable." Dale held his hands out wide, his fingers and nail beds caked with grime.

"Be reasonable?" Zoë chimed in. "How about this? You get that stream cleaned up by tomorrow afternoon, or I'm going to shut your timber operation down and levy a fine against your company that'll make your head spin."

Both men stared at her. Dale's eyebrows arched upward into his grimy hair, and he huffed great exhales of air.

She stood quiet, keeping her face completely calm, letting her words sink in. But she sure hoped he wouldn't call her bluff.

Dale turned to Tanner and his voice was almost a squawk. "Shutting us down would put a whole lotta people out of work. Are you gonna let her do that?"

A subtle smile creased the corners of Tanner's mouth. He met her eyes and she tried to read his mood, but could find no censure in his amber gaze. "Yes, Dale, I believe I'm in agreement this time. If you get the creek cleaned up, it won't be an issue. We'll forget it ever happened."

"Um, okay. We'll get it done." Dale patted the air with his hands, as if to soothe them.

"Thank you. We appreciate your cooperation." Zoë smiled sweetly and turned to go.

Without looking back, she walked to the Forest Service truck, got in and clicked on her seat belt. Her body trembled, but she knew deep inside that she'd done the right thing. She had no intention of shutting down this timber operation, but neither could she let them get away with this abuse. It was her job to protect the environment, and her boss in Portland would accept nothing less.

Tanner got into the truck, started the engine and drove down the dirt road without speaking. Zoë held on to the armrest like a lifeline. The dictates of her job wouldn't let her back down on this, but she didn't want Tanner mad at her for speaking out of turn. He'd supported her this time, his actions earning her respect. She couldn't explain why his approval mattered so much to her, but it did.

As soon as they were out of sight of the landing deck, Tanner pulled the truck over. He let the engine idle for a few moments as he sat there staring out the front window. A muscle ticked in his right cheek as he clenched his jaw. Zoë tensed and held her breath, determined not to lose her temper if he bawled her out.

"You know shutting down the timber operation would have put hundreds of people out of work, right?" He spoke thoughtfully, without looking at her.

"Yes, I know."

He looked at her, his dark eyes boring into hers like a high-powered drill. "Would you really have done that?"

Still a low, contemplative voice. She caught no censure in his tone. Just a genuine desire to know what she was thinking.

She thought about his question for a moment. The last thing she wanted was to cost the livelihoods of numerous families who were innocent of any wrongdoing. "No, of course not. I think the threat did the trick. We won't have to shut anyone down."

The tension in his face eased. "Good. I just wanted to know for sure."

"Why? This seems very important to you."

He rested one hand on his thigh, the other hand on the steering wheel. "It is. I wanted to know what kind of person you are. I'm glad you're not hard-hearted enough to put innocent people out of work in this rotten economy."

"No, I'm not. I know all those men working up there have families to feed. They're just doing what their bosses tell them to do, the same as you and me."

"I agree. The bosses were in the wrong. You won't receive an argument from me this time."

She froze for the count of three, then chuckled. "Well, this is a first. It seems we've finally agreed on something."

He glanced at her, a subtle doubt flashing in his eyes. She didn't move as he reached over and brushed a bit of sawdust off the sleeve of her shirt. The friendly gesture broke down the rigid wall of tension between them and she relaxed.

"Yeah, it does seem that way." He put the truck in gear and drove down the bumpy road. A wide grin flashed across his face. "I can't believe you got Dale to do what we asked. He usually fights me tooth and nail. Well done."

To save her life, she couldn't explain the pleasure his words gave her. A feeling of euphoria pulsed through her veins and she returned his smile. Finally, they'd found some common ground.

He shook his head in disbelief. "You've got grit. I'll give you that, Mrs. Lawton."

"Thank you," she said. "And please, call me Zoë."

He blinked, as though coming to his senses after being knocked loony with a baseball bat. His smile faded and she realized she'd said something wrong. But what? First he'd been happy with her; now he seemed irritated again. Did it have something to do with calling her by her first name? She couldn't imagine why that would be so offensive to him.

"You know, I'm a nice woman, Tanner," she said.

"That's just the problem." His voice dropped several octaves.

"I don't understand." She was sure getting mixed signals from this man.

"I know. I don't understand it myself. Let's just leave it at that, okay?" He didn't look at her as he spoke, but she caught an edge of regret in his gruff tone.

"Okay. We'll let it drop. But are we still on for fishing with Jonah on Saturday morning?"

She bit her bottom lip, wondering how she'd explain it to her son if Tanner decided not to take them. Even if she had to go shopping and buy the equipment and figure out how to use the poles herself, she was taking Jonah fishing.

Tanner glanced her way, a slow smile quirking one side of his mouth. "Of course. I wouldn't disappoint Jonah for anything in the world."

She released an inward sigh, thankful to Tanner in more ways than one. Whatever was causing his mood swings around her, at least he wasn't going to take it out on her son. "Thanks, Tanner. It means a lot to Jonah."

"I know."

And that was that. They drove most of the trip back into town in a comfortable silence. And when Tanner dropped her off in the parking lot so she could retrieve her car, the strain between them had eased.

"See you day after tomorrow," he said, a hesitant catch in his voice.

"We'll be ready."

She closed the truck door and stepped back so he could drive away. But he didn't move until she was safely buckled inside her car and had started the engine. It took her a few minutes to realize he was simply watching out for her. Making sure she was safe and her car worked properly before he left her alone.

A true sign of a gentleman.

It'd been a long time since anyone had watched out for her, and she kind of liked it. As she drove home, she couldn't help feeling as though she should have said something to make him feel better. It would help if she knew what was troubling him. But that meant getting more involved with him than she wanted to be. She liked Tanner Bohlman. She really did. But she sure didn't understand him.

Chapter Six

True to his word, Tanner arrived at Zoë's house promptly at nine on Saturday morning. Dressed in a pair of worn black jeans, a white T-shirt and scuffed boots, he looked casual and so handsome it made her throat ache. He hadn't shaved that morning, evidenced by the faint stubble on his chin. For some reason, that only added to his masculine appeal. When Zoë answered the door, she tried not to stare at his tousled hair and bright amber eyes.

"Good morning." He gave her that lopsided smile of his and stepped into the living room as she opened the door wide.

"Good morning," she said.

He eyed her denims and pink-painted toenails and a rush of panic flooded his face. "Aren't you coming with us?"

"Of course. I just need to put my shoes on." Until she knew him better, she'd never let Jonah go off alone with him.

"Okay, good." Tanner raked his fingers through his short hair, making it stand on end.

"He scares you that much?" She bit her bottom lip, forcing herself not to laugh.

A whoosh of air escaped Tanner's lungs and she realized she'd hit the nail on the head.

"It's just that I haven't been around little kids much. As long as you're with us, I shouldn't mess it up too badly. Besides, you need to learn how to fish, too."

Oh, this was good. Strong, in-control Tanner Bohlman scared of a little six-year-old boy.

"Coward," she teased and reached for her socks and shoes, which sat beside the front door.

He gave her a sheepish look, a half

smile curving his lips. "Does it show that much?"

She chuckled. "Just a bit."

He laughed, the deep sound of rolling thunder. It'd been a long time since she'd had an attractive man in her home, and she admitted to herself that she liked his presence here.

"Tanner!" Jonah came running down the hallway.

As the boy hugged the tall man's legs, an odd expression of fondness crossed Tanner's face. And that was when Zoë realized he wasn't immune to her little boy's charisma any more than she was.

"Hi, partner. You ready to go?" Tanner disengaged himself from the boy's arms and stepped back.

"Sure! Do I need anything else?" Jonah held out his arms to let Tanner inspect him, finding Jonah dressed much the same as he was.

"Nope, you look fine. Let's go."

Zoë grabbed her backpack and a jacket for her and one for Jonah before they piled into Tanner's truck. On the way to the fishing pond, an idea flashed through her mind and she gasped. "Oh, no! I forgot to get Jonah a fishing license."

Tanner reached up onto the dashboard and waved a small badge at her. "It's taken care of. He can catch six fish today."

"Thank you. Can I pay you for the license?"

"Nope. This is my treat."

"That's very kind of you." His consideration impressed her.

"Yeah, thanks, Tanner. This is the best summer ever." Jonah sat between them, happily bouncing his legs against the seat. He was so excited, he couldn't seem to sit still.

"You're welcome, buddy." Tanner ruffled the boy's blond hair.

They drove through town, then passed a tall, wooden sign that read Kids' Creek Park. The area looked like any other ordinary park, complete with a wide, grassy area where two children and their dog played Frisbee. Several covered picnic tables sat off to one side waiting for use. The pond itself wasn't large, but a solid wooden bridge spanned its width for traipsing back and forth to each side. Numerous kids stood on a wooden dock, casting their lines into the water. Tall cattails edged the shore where three gray ducks waddled around quacking and scavenging for food.

As they got out of the truck, Zoë nodded at the pond. "This is a great park for kids."

"Yeah, it's a safe, wholesome place to have fun," Tanner agreed.

Wholesome fun.

Zoë liked that. She figured teenagers could get into a lot more trouble than younger kids. As Jonah got older, a small-town environment might be better for him than a big city like Portland.

"Were you able to check Tilting Creek yesterday afternoon?" she asked.

Tanner nodded. "Yep, the logging operation cleaned up their mess. Not a bit of slash lying around in the buffer zone and the creek is running clear again."

"Good. Thank you so much." She was relieved to hear this news.

"No, thank *you*." He smiled into her eyes.

Liquid warmth pooled in the pit of Zoë's stomach. She felt odd and fuzzy inside. She liked being near this man and his lop-sided smile…when they weren't clashing over their work methods.

"This is your fishing pole." Tanner handed Jonah a short rod with a simple spinning reel. Tanner quickly showed the boy how to use it.

When Jonah looked at the pole, his face lit up as if it was Christmas morning. "This is great. Do I get to keep it?"

"Jonah! You're just borrowing it." Zoë gave her son a frown.

"It's okay." Tanner smiled at her before turning to look at Jonah. "Yes, you get to keep it. My gift to you. As long as it's okay with your mother."

"Can I keep it, please, Mom? Can I?"

They both looked at Zoë. She didn't have

the heart to deny the gift and she nodded her acquiescence. "Yes, of course."

Jonah's eyes widened with appreciation. "Thanks, Tanner. Now we can go fishing together all the time."

Zoë shook her head at Tanner. "You didn't need to do that."

Tanner shrugged as he shuffled through a tackle box, not meeting her eyes. "It's no problem. Really."

"At least let me pay you for it."

"There's no charge. It's the pole I used when I was a kid. It's one of the few things they let me keep in foster care. What else am I gonna do with it?"

She opened her mouth to mention the sentimental value he must feel for the fishing rod. Surely he'd want to give it to his own son one day. But then she thought better of it. Refusing the gift might lessen its value. Jonah needed the influence of a good man in his life, and she had no doubt her little boy would remember this day and his new fishing pole for the rest of his life.

"And this pole is for you." Tanner handed Zoë a longer black rod and reel.

"I...I didn't expect this."

He bent down and picked out a bright yellow lure and placed it in her hand. "You're a marine biologist. Don't you think it's time you learned how to fish?"

"Yes, I do." She couldn't help smiling with anticipation. She'd never thought about it before, but she liked how this man challenged and pushed her to try new things. After all these years of studying and working with fish, she'd finally get to catch her own.

"Now let's talk about bait." Tanner clapped his hands once and rubbed them together as though in anticipation.

Zoë didn't even flinch. Most women didn't like this yucky part of the process, but handling wriggling worms had never bothered her. "I can help, but isn't it illegal for me to catch fish in the kids' park?"

"Not if you catch and release them."

"Oh." A thrum of excitement whizzed through her. She wasn't in Portland anymore and she loved being outside all the time instead of sitting inside a stuffy lab.

Tanner rattled around in a small cooler chest, and she heard the faint sucking sound as he opened a plastic container. No doubt he was taking out worms.

"There's a special bait that rainbow trout can almost never resist." He looked over the lid of the cooler and winked at Zoë. "I'm about to share my trade secrets, so you've got to promise never to tell anyone else." He wagged his eyebrows at Jonah.

The boy giggled. "I promise not to tell."

"Me, either." Zoë chuckled, liking how Tanner interacted with her son. As though they were good friends.

"Shrimp!" Tanner held up a pink piece of deli shrimp between two of his long fingers.

"Shrimp? That's it?" Jonah's expectant expression wilted, replaced by a look of disappointment.

Tanner laughed, deep and low. "Believe me, it's enough to do the trick. Trout love shrimp."

The man reached for the hook on Jonah's line and leaned near as he showed the boy how to thread the shrimp from head to tail so it wouldn't come off easily. "Notice we're using a single, barbless hook. Do you know why?"

Tanner showed Jonah the difference between a barb and a hook and the child shook his head.

"It's because the barbs rip up the fish's mouth and do a lot of damage. Even if we catch and release the fish, it'll probably die later on. But a fish can survive a single-hook release pretty well."

"Oh." Jonah's brow crinkled in thought. "I don't want to hurt the fish. I just want to catch them."

Zoë gave her son a loving smile. "Unfortunately, it's impossible to not hurt the fish if you want to eat them later tonight."

"Don't worry. The fish in this pond are for eating. And eating fish is good for you," Tanner said.

Jonah's expression lightened and he

smiled, seemingly completely trusting of Tanner's explanation.

"Okay, let's go catch them." Tanner showed Jonah how to cast his line without hooking a person from behind. Once Jonah stood happily on the dock holding his fishing rod, Tanner turned his attention to Zoë.

Placing his hands on his hips, he eyed her with a subtle smile. "Do you need help hooking your shrimp?"

"No, thank you." She couldn't conceal the happy lilt in her voice. For a short time, she could forget about the lonely nights when Jonah was asleep and she prowled around her quiet house. She could pretend they were a normal, happy family out having fun together. She could forget they worked together and might yet need to deal with some difficult issues.

"Thanks for being kind to Jonah," she told him.

"You're welcome." Tanner handed her a piece of shrimp, his face flushing a light shade of pink.

Holding the rod firmly with her hands, Zoë pulled the hook forward and threaded it through the bait, just as she'd watched Tanner do. She pressed her tongue to her upper lip and concentrated to get it just right.

When she glanced up, she caught a look of surprise on his face. "What's wrong?"

He shook his head and smiled. "I've just never seen a woman hook her own bait before. You're...you're a bit different."

A laugh burst from her throat. "I hope that's good."

"Oh, it is, believe me. I think you're ready to go fishing."

She didn't need help to cast her line. But when Tanner touched her hand, a current of electricity surged beneath her skin. She couldn't remember the last time she'd had so much fun.

And when Jonah caught and landed his first fish, you'd have thought he'd cured cancer or something. Tanner wrapped his arm around Jonah's shoulders to help disengage the fish from the hook. The two of them laughed buoyantly, sharing a father-son moment that defied any need for explanation. And seeing them like this did something to Zoë's insides. She felt jittery, happy and sad all at the same time. She had to remind herself that she and Tanner weren't dating—that half the time he didn't even seem to like her. And even if they worked flat-out and tried for a relationship, it couldn't last. By the end of August, she and Jonah would return to Portland.

"I caught one. I really did it." Jonah hopped up and down with excitement.

Tanner chuckled as he helped the boy reel in the heavy fish. "Yes, you did. I'm proud of you, son."

Son. The word made Tanner pause. This wasn't his child. They were just friends, nothing more. He must remember that.

The line dragged forward, the slack going tight as the fish tugged on the hook. Finally, they saw the fish, skimming just below the surface as it thrashed around in the shallow water. And when they landed it on shore, Tanner understood why.

"Is this a rainbow trout?" Jonah skimmed his fingertips reverently across the smooth, shiny body.

"Nope, this is a steelhead. Like the rainbow trout, the steelhead has an orange-red stripe along its side. But its tail is squarer, its body more silvery." Tanner pointed out each of these characteristics for Jonah, teaching the boy lessons he'd remember the rest of his days.

Jonah laughed and touched the inky-black spots covering the fish's sides. "It's got freckles."

"Yep, it sure does." Tanner chuckled, enjoying himself thoroughly in spite of his promise not to bond with this little boy.

"It's so pretty." The boy watched the fish with awe.

"God has definitely made some beautiful creatures for our world," Zoë agreed.

Tanner stilled, listening intently to more than just the words spoken between mother and son. A feeling of reverence washed over him, so powerful that he couldn't deny his own amazement at God's creation. He vaguely remembered some tender moments with his own mom, who'd instilled an abiding conviction in him that the Lord had created the earth and every living creature in it. For His children.

For him.

As an adult, Tanner hadn't thought about God much. Since his grandparents died when he was just a kid, he'd been by himself. And being alone had hardened him in ways he couldn't even contemplate. He didn't trust or give his affection away easily, but once he did, he was loyal for life.

Maybe that was why his broken engagement with Cheryl hurt so much.

"This is the biggest fish I ever saw," Jonah exclaimed, an expression of pure rapture on his face.

"It is, huh?" Tanner knelt down and turned the fish on its back before disengaging the hook.

"Is this a seeded fish?"

Tanner nodded and held the steelhead

firmly, but gently, in his big hands. "Do you know how you can tell this is a hatchery-raised fish?"

"Uh-uh." The boy shook his head.

"See this area on the back of the fish, just in front of its tail?" Tanner pointed to the area, keeping the fish in the water to avoid duress in case Jonah decided to let it go.

"Yeah." Jonah's eyes widened, as if he were about to discover a miracle.

"There used to be a small adipose fin here. The hatchery snipped it off so we can tell if this is a wild or hatchery-raised fish."

Jonah puckered his lips. "Ah, the poor fish. Does it hurt?"

"I'm not a fish, so I don't know for sure. But I suspect it doesn't hurt more than stubbing your toe." Tanner liked the tender side of this little boy, but he also wanted to teach Jonah that it was okay to catch and eat fish.

"But why do we care if we can tell if the

fish is wild or came from a hatchery?" Jonah's eyes crinkled.

"Marking the adipose fin helps us count how many fish are wild, so we can determine if our efforts at preservation are working. If not, we have to decide on some other tactics to help the fish survive. You understand?"

The boy shook his head hard.

"Well, it's like this. Your mom takes you to get your measles and polio immunizations, right?" He glanced at Zoë, who stood close by, listening intently.

Jonah's eyes widened. "You mean my shots?"

"Exactly. They hurt, don't they?"

"Yes. A lot." Jonah rubbed his right shoulder, as if remembering his last injection.

"But your mom does it because she knows it'll help save your life. It'll keep you from getting an illness that might kill you. Even though it hurts, it's good for you."

Jonah glanced at his mother, who nodded. "I guess so."

"It's the same with the fish. If we don't clip their adipose fin, we wouldn't know if they were wild or hatchery-raised. And we need to know so we can help them survive."

Jonah's brows knit together as he thought this over. "Well, since we're trying to help the fish, I guess it's important to mark their fins."

"That's right. And yearling smolts are outplanted with their adipose fins clipped."

"What's a smolt?"

Tanner chuckled and glanced at Zoë, thinking he'd never finish answering questions with this curious little mind at work. "A smolt is a young fish about four to seven inches long. Even that small, the fish begins its migration toward the Pacific Ocean where it will grow into a big fish and be able to breathe in salt water."

"Migration?" Jonah prodded.

"That's when you travel long distances to live somewhere else," Zoë said.

Jonah nodded. "Like us! We migrated all the way from Portland to live here in Steelhead."

"Something like that," she agreed, ruffling the boy's hair with fondness.

Tanner smiled, liking the way Zoë patiently taught her son. Not once since knowing her had he ever heard her snap at the boy in anger.

"And you're trying to help save the fish, aren't you, Mom?" Jonah looked at his mother, his little chest thrust out with pride.

"Yes, I am."

"And Tanner, too." The boy rested his hand on Tanner's shoulder as the man knelt on the dock.

"Yes, Tanner, too," she said.

Zoë whipped out a camera from her pocket. Tanner tried to move away, but Jonah almost dropped the nineteen-inch fish. Tanner caught it in his bigger hands and the boy leaned close while Zoë snapped a couple of pictures.

A sugary-sweet feeling filled Tanner's

chest and he stood abruptly. A sensation of affection and confusion clogged his mind. He didn't want to have his picture taken with this cute little boy. He didn't want to love this child or enjoy Zoë's company. In fact, he wished Zoë were like most other women. Squeamish around worms and fish. Then he wouldn't like her so much. Being with her and Jonah left him feeling all mushy and soft inside.

"Can we eat our fish for dinner tonight?" Jonah gave a little skip, his body squirming with excitement.

"I guess so." Zoë spoke vaguely.

"Tanner can come over and eat it with us."

Zoë blinked and slid the camera back into her pocket. Tanner couldn't tell if she was indifferent or upset by Jonah's invitation.

"Sure, you're welcome to join us, Tanner. We'll eat about six," she said.

Mother and child looked at Tanner, waiting for his reply. He wanted to accept. He really did. But he'd spent so much time working with Zoë that he'd neglected his other assignments. He needed to get caught up.

"Sorry, but I can't make it tonight." He let a slow breath escape his lungs.

Jonah didn't bat an eye. "What about tomorrow?"

Tanner hesitated, swallowing, clenching his hands. "Sorry, partner. I can't."

Zoë's blue eyes crinkled with misgivings. Tanner could feel her gaze resting on him like a ten-ton sledge. In her expressive eyes, he saw her doubt. As though she sensed his uncertainty. And her sensitivity to his plight only made him more uncomfortable.

"Jonah, don't be pushy. Tanner has other plans," she said.

Tanner's hands shook. He looped his thumbs in his back pockets to keep Zoë from seeing the impact Jonah's invitation had on him. "Maybe some other time, okay?"

Jonah brightened at this idea. "Okay."

Tanner had done it now. Against all his

common sense, against his better judgment, he'd opened the corral gate and chased all the livestock out into the open. So to speak.

But maybe he was making too much of this. Sharing a meal with them now and then couldn't hurt. It didn't entail any long-term commitments. No falling in love. It was just dinner. Just food.

Wasn't it?

"Would you like to go to church with us in the morning?" Zoë asked.

"No!" He answered a bit too fast, but he couldn't help it. Sitting in church seemed too domestic. And anyway, he'd depended on himself for so long that he didn't need God anymore. The last thing he wanted was to be pressured into religion by a lovely widow and her son.

"Why don't we change spots and fish underneath that tree over there?" Tanner pointed across the pond, eager to put some distance between him and his fishing partners, if just for a few minutes.

"But we're catching fish over here," Jonah said.

"I know, but the sun is moving. It's casting our shadow onto the water. Fish know a shadow can mean a predator and they stay away. If we move, we'll have a better chance of catching your limit today."

And give Tanner a few minutes to calm his rattled nerves.

Without a word, Zoë reeled in her fishing line. Ignoring the leaf litter clinging to the hem of her blue jeans, she picked up the cooler and walked with her son across the bridge.

Jonah scurried ahead while Tanner carried the tackle box. The thud of Tanner's boots on the wooden planks mirrored the pounding of his pulse. He knew he should have canceled this fishing trip. Now it was too late. The damage was done.

"Jonah is so happy today. I can't thank you enough for taking the time to fish with us," Zoë said.

He couldn't respond. A lump the size of Kansas had lodged in his throat.

"Tanner, why aren't you married with a passel of your own kids?" she asked.

He swallowed hard and coughed, the blunt question catching him off guard.

"I'm sorry. That was rude of me to ask." Her cheeks flushed a delicate rose color.

"It's okay. Let's just say I wanted to be married, but it didn't work out."

"Yeah, for me, either. When Derek and I got married, we planned to have five children. We wanted enough for a basketball team." She gave a harsh laugh that revealed her disappointment.

Tanner's heart went out to her. Maybe she was the one woman that could understand his own heartache. "How long were you married before he died?"

"Two short years. But it was enough for us to love one another and to have Jonah. And that's something I'll never regret." She glanced Jonah's way, the wind ruffling her short hair as she gazed lovingly at her son.

Her words twisted inside Tanner's stomach. How he wished he could have known that kind of devotion with someone.

"Why haven't you remarried?" he asked.

She frowned. He'd turned the tables on her, and she didn't seem to like it.

"Truthfully?" she said.

"Truthfully."

She chewed the end of her pinkie finger, a characteristic he was fast learning meant she was pensive about something. "I've been so busy these past few years that it hasn't been a priority. I had Jonah, school and bills to worry about. Then I got busy with work, but I thrive on my career."

"Do you think you could ever love again?" Now, why did he ask that? He was digging deep here, being just as nosy as she'd been with him.

She met his eyes. "I hope so. It's taken a long time for my heart to heal, and I doubt I'll ever get over losing Derek. I don't think you can recover from that. But life is awfully lonely when you don't share it with someone else."

Tanner knew that firsthand. He wanted

to share his life, but he just hadn't met the right woman. Maybe he never would. And that thought left him feeling hollow and bereft.

Chapter Seven

The next morning, Zoë slept in later than usual. She didn't need to rush around before she and Jonah had to be at church at eleven. She enjoyed the slower pace. Standing inside her kitchen, she wore her fluffy bathrobe and blue slippers. Jonah was still asleep. She'd taken advantage of the opportunity to get a few things accomplished before he woke up.

Tidy packages of salmon filets rested on her countertop. She'd wrapped each steak in plastic and tin foil, to protect the meat from freezer burn. Tanner had been kind enough to clean Jonah's steelhead. All Zoë had needed to do was cut the meat into manageable sizes for broiling.

As she placed the filets into the freezer, she kept enough out for dinner that evening. She wished Tanner had accepted Jonah's invitation to join them.

Maybe she shouldn't have invited him to attend Sunday meetings with her and Jonah. As a diligent Christian, it was her job to do missionary work. She liked Tanner. A lot. But she also didn't want to appear pushy. They were coworkers, after all.

By eleven-fifteen, she and Jonah sat quietly on a pew inside the little chapel, listening to a sermon on keeping the Sabbath day holy. Though she tried to focus on the message, she felt encased by restless energy. Her thoughts kept returning to Tanner and the awesome day they'd spent together fishing. She'd see him tomorrow at the office and couldn't wait. Work had become more than a fun way to earn a living. With Tanner, it was an adventure she craved.

Following the meeting, she greeted Debbie Milan in the outer foyer. She'd met Debbie the first day she'd attended church.

"Hi, Zoë." Debbie waved as she shuffled her three young children down the hall to Sunday school class.

Zoë gave a friendly nod, enjoying the way Debbie's rosy cheeks plumped with her smile.

"Hi there, Billie." Jonah greeted Debbie's son, who was the same age as he was.

"Look what I got." Billie pulled a plastic snake from his pants pocket. With a bevy of shrill laughter, the two boys scurried down the hall, their heads close together.

"Billie!" Debbie called after her son, but it did no good. The boys moved too fast for their moms to catch them.

Debbie shook her head. "There goes madness and mayhem. I feel sorry for their poor Sunday school teacher today."

Zoë bit her bottom lip and tried not to laugh, hoping Jonah behaved. "I guess we'll have to rename them the Trouble Twins."

"That's a good name for our boys. I keep trying to remember they'll grow up to be fine, upstanding men one day. But in the meantime…" Debbie shifted the heavy weight of her book bag, ignoring the impatient tug of her toddler on her hand. "Hey, you play the piano, don't you, Zoë?"

Zoë bent down and picked up the baby, trying to help ease Debbie's load just a bit. "Yes, although I'm sadly out of practice."

"Millie Archer isn't here today. Would you mind playing for the children's singing time?"

Pleased by the invitation, Zoë nodded. "Sure, as long as you're willing to tolerate a wrong note or two. I haven't had time to play for several months. I left my piano in Portland."

"You'll do fine. The alternative is for me to play, which would be very scary. I can only play the top notes of the music." The two women laughed together as they made their way down the hall.

"Looks like you've got your hands full anyway." Zoë couldn't help admiring Debbie, who seemed to volunteer for everything, in addition to juggling her three kids and a thriving home-based mail-order business.

"I know you have a busy day job, too," Debbie said. "But Billie's been harping at me to invite Jonah over. Would that work for you?"

Zoë had been thinking about how to broach this very topic. "Absolutely. Jonah's been asking the same thing. Why don't you bring Billie to my house?"

They agreed on a day and time.

"You could leave Mindy and Shane with me, too." Zoë hugged the baby in her arms. She'd be busy watching four little kids, but she didn't mind. She'd always hoped to have more children. Now she wondered if she'd ever get the chance.

"Oh, that'd be too much," Debbie said.

"No, it wouldn't. And it'd give you a break."

Debbie hesitated. "Okay, but just for two

hours. I can get my grocery shopping done without any distractions and then I'll come rescue you."

The two women chuckled and Zoë breathed a sigh of delight. More and more, she and Jonah were feeling right at home in this community. They had friends. They were happy for the first time in a long time.

And then the summer would end.

As Zoë sat in front of the piano during singing time, she couldn't help wondering where Tanner was this morning. What was he doing today? And how could she help him not be estranged from God?

Not her business. But she'd still come to care for Tanner in a friendly sort of way. Maybe in the future she'd have the opportunity to casually bring up the topic again. She wasn't the answer to anyone's problems, but maybe she could influence Tanner to give the Lord one more try.

Following the meeting, Zoë stood in the foyer waiting for Jonah to get out of class when Paul Carter approached her.

He was a tall, handsome man in a pretty sort of way. Even when he was serious, however, he seemed to always wear a perpetual grin with big, white teeth that Zoë found mildly irritating. It wasn't logical, but the man gave her the creeps.

"Hi, Zoë. Did you get the information about our father-son outing? We're going up to Camp Fleshermann for the day. There'll be lots of games, food and activities for the boys." He handed her a flyer to advertise the event coming up in two weeks.

"I'd heard about it but didn't know the details." She stepped back when he brushed his hand against her arm. It was a friendly gesture, but it didn't feel right to her. He seemed too clingy, considering they'd only met last week.

"Since Jonah doesn't have a dad, I'd be happy to be his father for the day." Again the toothy smile widened Paul's mouth like a giant clown face.

Zoë forced herself to meet his eyes. Paul was a single father of two sons. Debbie had mentioned that he'd been divorced twice now and had visitation of his sons on the weekends. The boys each had different moms. Zoë didn't want to be wife number three.

She kept her voice kind as she responded in an even tone. "You're so nice to offer, but I don't even know if Jonah will be able to go on the outing that day."

"Oh. Okay. I'll check back with you next Sunday. It should be lots of fun."

Paul crowded closer, invading her personal space. She caught the cloying scent of his heavy cologne and held her breath. She couldn't help comparing him to Tanner, who always had a light, spicy smell.

When Paul reached up and rubbed her shoulder, Zoë almost bolted. She stepped sideways, wishing he'd stop touching her. She found the man repulsive. She just didn't get a good feeling around him. He kept coming and she almost tripped over a garbage can in her quest to move away.

Paul rounded the can, following her every move like a stealth bomber. "If you decide Jonah's going to attend, I'd be happy to pick him up and take—"

"There's Jonah." She hurried toward her son, hating herself for being rude. But an overwhelming feeling of distaste had forced her to get out of this conversation right now.

"Okay, then. Talk to you later," she heard Paul call to her retreating back.

"Mom! Look what I got." Jonah held up a picture he'd colored of the ancient prophet Noah. A large brown blob had to be the ark. The giraffes were unmistakable, with long, orange necks and bushy tails.

"That's wonderful, sweetie." Zoë knelt beside her son, focusing her attention entirely on him. Hoping Paul took the hint and went about his business.

No such luck. When she stood and took Jonah's hand, Paul still hovered beside the front door like a hawk perched over a field mouse. Although it meant walking around the entire building to get to her car, Zoë pulled Jonah with her and ducked out the back door.

For just a moment, Zoë wished Tanner were here. Paul wouldn't crowd so close if the fish-and-wildlife specialist were standing nearby. Tanner didn't swarm her or invade her space. She felt relaxed when he was around.

Protected.

"What's the hurry? Why are we going around the long way?" Jonah asked, his little legs moving fast to keep up.

"This way we can enjoy the sunny day," she said.

Inside her car, she drove them home and wondered what to do about a father for Jonah on the upcoming outing. Maybe Blaine, Debbie's husband, wouldn't mind chaperoning Jonah for the day along with Billie. It was a logical fix to her problem. She liked Blaine well enough and he seemed to like Jonah. There'd be lots of other fathers and their sons of all ages present. It was just a day trip; no sleepover in a tent. And it'd be good for Jonah to get out and be with the other kids.

And yet, Zoë kept thinking about Tanner and the way he'd taught Jonah to fish. His deep laughter as he patiently disengaged the hook from his pant leg after Jonah had caught it there by accident. The way his expressive eyes lit up with amusement when Jonah decided to let all but one fish swim free.

She wanted to ask Tanner to accompany her son on the outing, but getting him to take her boy on a daylong, church-sponsored activity might be pushing things too far. And too fast.

She just couldn't do it.

As she pulled into her driveway at home, Zoë thought about the brown rice, fresh broccoli, fruit salad and ice-cream sundaes she'd planned to accompany their fish for dinner. She wished Tanner would be joining them. He'd made it clear he didn't want anything to do with God, but surely he wouldn't object to a father-son outing. Would he?

Funny how she'd come to trust Tanner so quickly. In spite of the differences in their approach to work, she felt as though she'd known him forever. They had a lot in common. And they'd found ways to get along together. Tanner was also fun to be with. Any woman would be lucky to—

No! She wasn't any woman. She came with a lot of baggage. A dead husband and a six-year-old son. And maybe that wasn't fair to Tanner. Maybe he didn't want to be a father to Jonah.

If that were true, he was very good at hiding it. He seemed like a natural dad.

She'd wait until she saw Tanner again. Maybe the opportunity would arise for her to bring up the topic of the father-son outing. He might even volunteer to accompany Jonah. The worst he could say was no. In that event, she'd move to Plan B and ask Blaine to take her boy.

She hoped her plan worked.

Tanner was a coward. He admitted it freely to himself. He should have agreed to have dinner with Zoë and Jonah tonight. But being around Zoë had completely shattered his composure. He'd fallen hook, line and sinker for her little son. And he was fast falling for her, too.

He looked down at the crumpled piece of paper in his hand. The one Zoë had given him weeks ago with her cell-phone number scrawled beneath her name. Even though she was a coworker, he was seriously considering asking her out on a real date. What could it hurt? Tomorrow afternoon when he drove her out to look at Red Creek, he'd ask her to dinner on Friday night. That should give her time to schedule a babysitter for Jonah.

With his mind made up, Tanner sat on the lumpy sofa in his apartment and worked on some watershed reports. Two hours later, he stared blankly at a ball game on TV, not even aware of who was playing or the score.

He missed Zoë. He missed Jonah. And he was hungry. And sick and tired of microwave meals. He should have gone over to their house tonight. He should have tickled Jonah, laughed, had a good time and then helped Zoë wash the dishes after supper. Then they could have sat together and watched TV while Jonah played in the background. Tanner might have even reached over and held Zoë's hand. Or wrapped his arm around her shoulders.

Like a real family.

He had a big dilemma on his hands. He liked Zoë. Liked her a lot.

One thought sustained him. He'd see her tomorrow afternoon. And he couldn't wait.

His plans to ask Zoë out on a date changed abruptly the next morning. Chuck Daniels, the forest supervisor, stuck his head inside Tanner's office first thing.

"You got a minute to meet in my office?"

"Sure." Tanner stood and followed his boss down the hall.

"What's up?" Tanner asked as he closed the door and sat facing Chuck across a wide mahogany desk.

Chuck frowned as he tossed three pink slips toward Tanner. Phone messages with names and numbers scrawled across them. "I spent Friday afternoon returning angry phone calls from three local farmers."

Tanner picked up the papers and glanced through them. Harry Ragsdale's name was among them.

Chuck didn't wait for Tanner to respond. "It seems that our new fishery biologist has been ruffling some feathers with her demands."

Oh, no. Tanner had been afraid of this. But he thought the situation had been handled. So why had the farmers complained? "Zoë made it clear what was expected of the farmers, but each of them agreed to let us install a screen on their property. She was never rude to any of them. I don't know why they called you."

The leather chair creaked as Chuck sat back and glared. Tanner could almost see steam spewing out of his nose and ears. "What exactly did she say to them?"

Tanner recalled the dialogue as best he

could, then shrugged, trying to lighten the moment. He knew the last thing the forest supervisor wanted was a bunch of phone calls from angry farmers. "She just did her job, Chuck. It wasn't a big deal. This is nonsense."

Chuck leaned forward, his gray eyes narrowed. "Look, Tanner. I don't want Zoë Lawton upsetting the local farmers so I end up with a bunch of picketers parading outside my office. And I don't want to see my name on the five-o'clock news or in the newspaper, either. Got it?"

Something hardened inside Tanner. He couldn't explain why, but he felt compelled to defend Zoë. "The farmers we met with have obviously spoken to each other. They're being unreasonable. We worked everything out with them and they were satisfied. For them to call and complain like this, I have to believe they just want to make trouble."

"I don't care what their reasons are. I don't want them calling me about this again. You keep that woman in line.

You're her chaperone for this summer fishery project. You take care of it."

Tanner couldn't believe this request. It was completely out of line, but Chuck was his boss. Tanner liked Zoë, but he also loved his job. He didn't want to do anything to jeopardize his future promotions. "And just how do you expect me to keep her in line? I'm not her boss, Chuck. We have no control over her. She works for a different agency. And besides, she's doing the job she was sent here to do. I can find no fault with her."

Chuck blew out a harsh breath, his features softening just a bit as he listened to reason. "You're right. Besides, we only have to deal with her for the summer. Humor her over the next eight weeks, but keep her from making waves. She'll be leaving at the end of August to go back to Portland. Just keep her in line until then and we'll be fine."

Tanner's heart dropped to the floor and something went cold inside him. "What do you mean she's leaving? I thought she'd been transferred here to Steelhead."

"Not permanently. This is just a summer work project for her. Because she's got a kid, she only accepted this assignment as long as it wouldn't interfere with her son's schooling. She'll be going back to Portland before school starts in the fall, and I say good riddance."

A war of emotions invaded Tanner's mind. No one had told him Zoë was here just for the summer. Because she worked for the National Marine Fisheries Service, he wasn't fully in the loop on information like that. Zoë hadn't mentioned it, but then it really wasn't his business. He liked her and Jonah. He wanted to spend time with them. A lot of time. And yet, the same dilemma that had haunted him all his life now reared its ugly head.

He was developing feelings for someone he couldn't be with long-term.

A heavy weight settled in his stomach. The thought of saying goodbye to Zoë and Jonah left him feeling rotten and grouchy inside. He had his career here in Steelhead and she had hers in Portland. A long-distance relationship would never work between them.

So much for asking her out on a date.

"I'll do my best to soften her demands with the farmers. It shouldn't be an issue anymore," Tanner promised.

"Good." Chuck nodded, as if that was settled.

As Tanner stood and returned to his own office, he felt a deep sense of loss. He didn't like the subterfuge his boss demanded from him. It wasn't right to just humor Zoë. She'd proven herself, and she knew what she was doing. But Tanner didn't want to jeopardize his own career.

Neither did he like the idea of Zoë returning to Portland. He'd only known her a short time. Surely this empty feeling had nothing to do with her and Jonah leaving in August. It had nothing to do with never seeing them again.

Or did it?

Tanner made an excuse not to work

with Zoë that afternoon. He needed time to think. To put some distance between them.

As he sat at his desk, he couldn't resist the urge to go online and check the job listings from the Portland regional office. His throat tightened when he saw a position for a fisheries biologist. It'd be a slight demotion, but he could fill the position easily enough…if he accepted a transfer to leave Steelhead.

Which he wouldn't. Not yet. He was just…exploring other opportunities. No harm in that.

With that in mind, he called up the job description. He decided to apply for it without telling anyone. He might or might not get it. What did he have to lose?

Nothing but his heart.

Chapter Eight

Four days later, Tanner parked his truck near the entrance of the Fish and Wildlife Office before walking up the front steps of the redbrick building. The United States flag whipped in the summer breeze, a cluster of yellow marigolds surrounding the tall pole. He'd been here so many times, it felt like a second home. But maybe he shouldn't have come today.

Inside, the reception lobby was empty with a sign on the front counter that said Ring Bell.

Ignoring the bell, Tanner walked toward the back laboratory where he figured Zoë might be working. Either that or in her tidy office. He'd visited her here on numerous occasions, dealing with their work issues, consulting about samples she'd taken or to schedule their next road trip up into the mountains.

He tried to tell himself today was no different. He was here on business, nothing more.

As he approached the lab, his pulse sped up. The light was on, and he peered past the desk at the microscopes, bins for holding fish and the tall refrigerator against the wall. No one was there, the pristine counters showing no signs of work today. Instead, he turned and took the stairs two at a time. His stomach churned as he neared her office, his steps faltering. He couldn't explain his intense desire to see her.

The clicking sounds of someone typing on a keyboard and business chatter in one of the offices filtered through the air. As he neared her door, he didn't know what to say. He couldn't ask her out, so he'd just schedule their next road trip.

The unmistakable voice of a little boy

echoed down the hall, followed by a *thud-thud* like something soft hitting the floor.

"Jonah, please don't bounce your ball inside the building. Wait until we get outside." As usual, Zoë's tone sounded calm and unruffled.

Just hearing her voice settled Tanner's nerves a smidgen. But Jonah was here. Inside his mother's office right now.

Tanner froze in midstride. He glanced at his wristwatch and realized it was late afternoon. For some reason, Zoë must have picked Jonah up early from his child-care provider. It was one thing for Tanner to work with Zoë, but he didn't want to face her son again.

Tanner pivoted on his heels, ready to head back the way he'd come and make a quick getaway. He could do this another time. Or call. Or better yet, just send Zoë an email.

"Tanner!" Jonah's voice filled the hallway like a shout.

Tilting his head, Tanner saw the boy

standing outside his mother's office door, clutching a large red ball to his chest.

"Hi, partner." Tanner was caught—no use in trying to run now.

He walked the few yards to the door and went inside the office with Jonah. The little boy slipped his hand inside Tanner's and held tight, grinning wide. As he enfolded Jonah's warm fingers with his own, Tanner's heart gave a hard squeeze.

Zoë stood in front of her computer, dressed in blue jeans. Her white blouse and turquoise jacket darkened the color of her eyes. Casual, yet professional. Her spiky hairstyle accented her pixie face and suited her spunky personality. Tanner thought she was the most beautiful woman he'd ever seen.

She held her purse in one hand, the computer mouse in the other, getting ready to leave.

"Hi, Tanner." She glanced up and flashed that dazzling smile of hers.

"You on your way out?" he asked.

"Yeah, we're driving over to pick up the

Milan kids. We're having a playdate at our house this afternoon."

Tanner's stomach gave an odd little twist. For just a moment, he wished he could join them. The thought of playing football or going fishing with Jonah brought him a strange sense of contentment. He had to keep reminding himself he wasn't Jonah's father and this wasn't his family. And he preferred it that way.

Of course he did.

"There. I've shut my computer down and we're ready to go." She stepped around her desk, pulling the strap of her purse up over her shoulder.

Tanner lifted a hand to indicate the hallway. "I just thought I'd stop by and say hi."

Okay, it was an excuse. A barrier to protect his own heart. Until he'd seen her, he'd had half a mind to ignore his resolve not to get any closer and ask her if he could take her and Jonah out for dinner tonight. Now he couldn't get the words past his constricted throat.

Jonah bounced the ball one more time, letting it roll across the flat carpet until it bumped against the opposite wall. "Hey, Tanner, will you be my daddy?"

Tanner's mouth dropped open in surprise. The air left his lungs in a quick whoosh and he felt as though he'd been slugged in the gut.

"Jonah!" Zoë looked at her son as if he'd just slapped her, too.

"Um, what do you mean?" Tanner almost choked on the words. How he wished he could be this boy's father. But that would mean he'd have to be Zoë's husband. And that was impossible under the circumstances.

"For the father-son outing. I need a dad to go with me." The boy smiled happily, completely unaware of the consternation his request had caused the adults in the room.

"The father-son outing?" Tanner clenched his hands, finding them slightly damp. He looked at Zoë for help.

She hitched one shoulder and gave him

an apologetic frown before speaking to Jonah. "Remember we talked about this, hon. I'm going to see if you can go with Blaine. If he can't take you, Paul has offered to do so."

"But I don't want Blaine or Paul to take me. I want to go with Tanner."

"Do you mean Blaine Milan, by chance?" Tanner asked.

Zoë nodded, her face slightly red with embarrassment. Her son's candor obviously upset her. "Yes, do you know him?"

"Very well. He owns Milan's Gas Station downtown. We have a contract to buy our fuel from him. From what I've seen, he's a good man."

"Yes, his wife, Debbie, and I have become very good friends. Jonah plays with their son Billie all the time. I'm sorry, Tanner. I didn't know Jonah was going to ask you to do this. He's just a kid and doesn't always think things through before he jumps in with both feet."

Yeah, a cute little kid that Tanner had

grown to love in spite of his vow never to do so.

"Can't your mom take you?" Tanner asked Jonah.

"Of course not! She's a girl. This outing is just for us guys." Jonah's nose crinkled with repugnance, as if his point was obvious to everyone.

"And what is this you want me to take you to again?" Tanner felt cornered and uncertain.

Zoë quickly explained about the day-long outing at Camp Fleshermann, located in the mountains about sixty miles outside of town. She then pointed out to Jonah that the church had made a point of advising parents that no boy would be turned away because he didn't have a father. They had plenty of men who would "adopt" a son for the day. No one would be left behind. But that didn't seem good enough for Jonah.

"Paul doesn't really like me. He only offered because he wants to date Mom," Jonah told Tanner.

Zoë gasped. "Jonah!"

"Well, it's true. And you told me not to lie."

Her eyes narrowed, her voice slightly scolding. "Paul's never asked me out."

"Not yet. But everyone's talking about it at church, Mom. He'll ask you, just wait and see."

Zoë's eyes widened in shock. "What do you mean everyone's talking about it?"

"I heard Tim and Josh talking about it," Jonah explained. "Tim and Josh are Paul's sons, so they know who their dad wants to date."

Zoë's mouth hardened. "Well, don't worry about it. I get the last word on the matter. Paul hasn't asked me out, and if he does—"

She let the thought hang, but Tanner admitted he liked her negative tone. He sensed that she didn't like this Paul fellow, which suited Tanner just fine.

"Good. I don't like Paul," Jonah said.

Neither did Tanner, though he had no reason not to. After all, Tanner had never met the guy. And he would have laughed if he hadn't been feeling so territorial. Though he had no right to interfere, Tanner didn't want Zoë going out with other men, which wasn't logical. She had a right to date and be happy, especially if he didn't intend to ask her out. "And this event is sponsored by your church?"

Dragging her gaze away from her son, Zoë nodded.

"I want you to go out with Tanner. I want him to take me on the father-son outing." Jonah jerked his thumb at Tanner, speaking to his mother as though Tanner weren't standing right there listening to every word.

Zoë tossed her head with an embarrassed laugh. "Let's talk about it later when we get home."

The room seemed to close in on Tanner. He felt overheated in spite of the cool breeze whisking past his face from the air conditioner.

"But, Mom—"

Zoë rested a hand on her hip and scowled

at her son. "Jonah Aaron Lawton, we will have this discussion in private at home. Got it?"

As if sensing that he'd pushed his mother too far, Jonah nodded, not looking any too happy about it. His response showed his true feelings. "Yes, I got it!"

The boy brushed past Tanner and ran down the hall to the stairwell.

"Jonah!" Zoë went after her son, pausing when she saw him leaning against the wall and glaring down at the gray carpet. Now and then, he tossed an angry look at his mom.

Tanner stood just behind Zoë, feeling out of place. Undoubtedly, this church outing meant a lot to the boy. But what could Tanner do about it?

Zoë released a pensive sigh, her eyes meeting Tanner's. "I'm so sorry about this. I didn't know Jonah was going to bushwhack you or that he'd overheard things like that at church. He was out of line to—"

"It's okay, Zoë." Tanner had heard enough.

How bad could the outing be? He already knew a number of the dads, including Blaine Milan and Terry Sadler. It was a small community and they weren't strangers to him.

"I just don't want you to feel obligated," she said.

Tanner took a deep inhale. "If it means that much to Jonah, I'll take him."

Now he'd done it. He couldn't believe he'd agreed. It seemed he had no self-control as far as Jonah was concerned. Before her death, Tanner's mom had dated a few men he hadn't liked. And Tanner didn't want Jonah going through that. Or Zoë, for that matter. She deserved so much better. She deserved a man like—

Who? Him?

Yes! No!

Oh, he didn't know anymore.

Tanner looked away, trying to settle his raw nerves. If nothing else, Zoë wouldn't be with them on the outing. It was just for the men and boys. Tanner could ensure Jonah had a good time, kind of like a big-brother thing. It didn't include any uncomfortable commitments. Just a fun day together. Right?

Of course right.

"You don't need to take him," Zoë said. "Blaine can take Jonah. They should do just fine together and I know how much you dislike religion."

Tanner quirked one brow. "I never said I had anything against religion. It's just that… There's not gonna be a lot of religious stuff, is there? It's only a day outing of activities?"

"Yes, they're going to play games, make fun crafts, have a barbecue, go fishing, things like that. But in all honesty, they're also having a morning devotional to start the day off right. It'll include prayer. So, yes, God will be a part of it, too."

He figured as much. But he appreciated her honesty, something he'd never had from Cheryl. He could handle a day outing just fine. Before his grandfather had died, he'd taken Tanner to a few of these types of church outings. And Tanner had loved every minute of them. The hiking, swimming, fishing and games. Even the devotionals. And his grandpa's deep baritone voice as he sang the hymns. Once Tanner went into foster care, all that ended. Tanner wanted more for Jonah. To have good, clean fun. To laugh and build relationships with the other boys. To create wonderful lifelong memories that would sustain him during difficult times ahead.

With him. Not with Paul or even Blaine.

"I'll take him." And Tanner meant it. He really wanted to go, for better or worse. He just hoped he wouldn't regret it later on.

Zoë peered at Tanner as if he'd lost his mind. "Are you absolutely sure you want to take Jonah to the father-son outing?"

A heavy weight settled in the pit of her stomach. She didn't feel good about this. Tanner had been her choice to take Jonah all along, but she was also highly conscious of how Tanner felt about God. Prayer and faith were so important to Zoë, and it hurt her deeply that Tanner wanted nothing to do with them in his life.

"Yep, I'm sure." He gave her a slow smile that turned her heart to mush.

"I'd like you to take him, but…"

"But what? You prefer Paul over me?"

"No, of course not! I mean, yes." She hesitated, hoping he wouldn't get the wrong idea. "No. That's not it at all."

"Then what?" He tilted his head in that tolerant manner of his that told her he was genuinely interested in what she had to say. His expressive eyes narrowed on her face, looking deep inside her soul.

"It's just that the Lord means everything to me, Tanner. He's the basis of my life. Him and Jonah. And I don't want anything to damage that for my son."

"I understand that, but what are you getting at?" He spoke softly, his jaw clenched.

"I…I don't want you to say anything to Jonah that might make him feel the way you do about God." Okay, she'd blurted it out, but she had to be truthful with Tanner. She couldn't pretend. Not about this. It was too important to her.

Tanner clamped his mouth tight, his eyes hardening. "I would never do that, Zoë. Not ever."

"Maybe not intentionally, but your feelings might come out in other ways."

"What ways?"

"I don't know." She shook her head in frustration. An icy fist clutched her heart. She hated insulting this kind man or making him feel inept in any way. But she was Jonah's mother and she had to put her child's well-being above everything else. She had to be sure Tanner wouldn't do or say anything to damage her son's faith. She had to raise her child as she saw fit. And no one else had a right to undermine her efforts, even if it was done innocently enough.

A flash of pain filled Tanner's eyes, then was gone. So fast that she thought she'd imagined it. But she knew better. She'd hurt him. Deeply. After he'd been so kind to her and Jonah.

Tanner's voice sounded gruff with emotion. "I appreciate your honesty more than I can say. But I won't include my personal feelings about God in my conversations with Jonah. Not ever."

"What happened to make you so indifferent to God?" She shouldn't inquire into his personal business. She had no right. And yet, she felt compelled to ask.

"I got dumped. By my fiancée. Just weeks before the wedding. I learned my lesson. End of story." He gave a harsh laugh, as though trying to brush it off. But she wasn't fooled. Not one bit.

"How long ago was this?"

He looked away. "Just over two years."

"And you blame God?"

"Not really. It was Cheryl's fault. And mine. I never should have trusted her."

He sounded so cynical and pessimistic. And Zoë couldn't help wondering if that was why he seemed to fight getting closer to her. Because he'd been hurt. Because he didn't trust her. Or was it because he didn't trust all women?

"Then you believe in God. You're just angry at Him." She made it a statement, not a question.

"I guess so. God kind of became a casualty in my life. I've lost everyone that ever meant anything to me, so I stopped trusting Him. I figured I didn't need the Lord anymore, either." He glanced down the hallway at the door to the stairwell, as though he longed to escape.

"Believe me, I understand that feeling." She spoke in a kind tone, trying to put him at ease. "After Derek died, I was so angry at God. I had a new baby to raise without a father. I couldn't figure out why the Lord would take my husband when we needed him so desperately."

"Yeah, that'd be pretty bad," he agreed.

"But then some wonderful things happened in my life. Somehow I pulled good grades in school with very little sleep. I got scholarships and a new job with a supportive boss who allowed me to study when I wasn't busy with work. I found a fabulous babysitter who loved and cared for Jonah. The Lord took my husband, but He stayed with me while I figured out my life. It hasn't been easy, but I've never felt alone or abandoned. Not once. And I'm stronger because of it. I don't know why God took Derek, but I know it must be for my betterment. I believe there were lessons I needed to learn and the Lord knew this was the best way for that to happen. Sometime down the road, I'll understand. I just have to trust that God has my best interests at heart."

Tanner blinked at her, as though digesting what she'd said. As though he didn't quite believe her.

"Your faith amazes me. If anyone has a right to turn away from God, you do," he said.

She caught not a single hint of sarcasm in his tone. But maybe she'd told him too much. He'd always been so easy to talk to, in spite of their rough beginning. In spite of their different work methods. She just wished they could be—

What?

More than friends. She didn't dare confide that longing, even to herself. At least not out loud. Falling for this man should be the last thing on her mind right now. She had her work to do and then she'd take Jonah back to Portland.

"I appreciate your telling me these things," he said. "Really, I do. But it doesn't change anything for me."

What else could he say? She'd unloaded a lot on him, without his even asking. Confiding in each other wasn't going to heal his injured soul. It'd take time and a lot of faith to do that.

"So, are you gonna let me take Jonah to the father-son outing?"

His words helped her slough off the glum mood she'd fallen into. In spite of everything, Tanner still wanted to take Jonah.

She chuckled. "Of course. He told me last night that, except for Billie and me, you're his best friend. I don't think you'll ever know how much that fishing trip meant to him."

"Oh, I think I've got a pretty good idea." He showed a warm smile of understanding.

"You and I have worked quite a bit together and I trust you with my most prized possession, Tanner. But don't you think it's time you let your anger at the Lord go?"

The blood drained from his face, as though she'd slapped him. He stared deeply into her eyes, as though he could read her thoughts. Rather than turning away, he reached out and brushed a short wisp of hair back from her cheek. The warmth of his fingers against her skin sent a zing of electricity through her.

Did he feel it, too?

"My dear Ms. Lawton, I think you should mind your own business." His voice sounded low and composed, not a smidgen of anger to be heard.

Okay, he'd put her in her place quite gently. She had no right to interfere. She must accept that. But she couldn't help worrying about him. And wishing he could feel the way she did about God.

He stepped back, breaking the moment. She almost sagged against the wall, wondering why this man had such a strong impact on her. He stood there wearing his Forest Service uniform, looking tall and handsome and in control.

Her knees wobbled and her arms felt weak. Being close to Tanner made her feel all quivery inside. But she was in danger of crossing barrier lines. She realized that neither she nor Tanner could allow that to happen. They both carried too much extra baggage to let down their guard easily. And even if they let each other in, their relationship wouldn't last very long into the future.

"What time should I pick Jonah up?" Tanner smiled as he slung his thumbs into the pockets of his green Forest Service pants.

Somehow she mumbled the information, then waited for his confirming nod. Their deep conversation was over. Time to move on to normal, everyday life again.

"You can count on me," he said.

Oh, I certainly hope so.

The thought came unbidden to her mind, startling her with its intensity. She'd been so strong for so long that she didn't dare count on anyone but herself and God. Maybe that could change now. Maybe she'd learned what the Lord wanted her to know, and now He wanted her to learn something else.

Like how to love again.

As Tanner turned and walked down the hallway toward Jonah, Zoë stood there, frozen to the floor. Tanner paused and spoke to her son for just a moment. His deep voice filtered through the air, but she couldn't make out his words. In response, Jonah's happy yell made her blink. Obviously, Tanner had told the boy that he would take him on the father-son outing. Jonah had gotten his way.

Zoë realized how much she missed being able to rely on a man's strength when she needed his help around the house. Or when she felt blue and had no one but the Lord to confide her troubles to.

Not since her husband had Zoë felt physically, mentally or spiritually drawn to another man. But why did it have to be Tanner Bohlman who made her heart sing?

It didn't seem to matter that she'd be leaving at the end of August or that Tanner didn't have faith in God. Whether she liked it or not, whether she was ready or not, she was falling for Tanner Bohlman. Hook. Line. And sinker.

Chapter Nine

"So you work with Zoë Lawton?"

"Yes, that's right." Tanner didn't look up, concentrating instead on the long, thin sticks of pine he'd been whittling with his pocketknife. He'd been hammered with questions from the man sitting next to him since he and Jonah arrived at Camp Fleshermann four hours earlier.

Paul Carter. The man Jonah hadn't wanted to take him on the father-son outing.

Trying not to be rude, Tanner continued peeling the outer bark off the sticks, then chiseled a sharp point on their ends. Almost done now. Then he and Jonah could pierce their hot dogs and roast them over the campfire.

Paul shifted his seat on the enormous fallen tree trunk, preparing a stick for himself. As much as he tried, Tanner couldn't seem to get rid of the guy or figure out why Paul had made him his new best friend. Obviously, Paul was interested in Zoë, but why did he keep questioning Tanner about her? The incessant inquiries irritated Tanner—no denying it.

Laughter and a cacophony of male voices filled the air. Structured chaos settled over the picnic area as approximately thirty fathers and their sons, ranging from toddlers to teenagers, milled around in preparation for their noon meal. Everyone was having fun.

Except Paul's sons. The two boys sat off to one side, trying to prepare their own hot-dog sticks. One of them, a gangly kid, perhaps eleven years old, came over and stood beside his father.

"My knife's too dull, Dad. Can you sharpen my stick for me?"

"Nah, you can do it. Keep at it." Paul brushed the boy aside before focusing back on Tanner. "Do you spend a lot of time with Zoë?"

"I work with her, so we see each other several times a week."

"Have you ever gone out with her?" Paul's small eyes narrowed as he waited for Tanner's response.

"You mean on a date?"

"Yeah."

"Nope." Tanner waved the sticks in the air to get Jonah's attention.

The boy stopped chasing Billie Milan and came running. He stumbled over a rock along the way, catching himself just before he went sprawling in the pine needles littering the ground.

"Whoa! You okay?" Tanner clutched the child's arm, his heart beating fast. He'd feel rotten if he had to explain to Zoë that Jonah had gotten hurt while in his care.

"Yeah, I'm fine." Jonah sounded breathless with excitement.

Tanner chuckled, figuring the boy would

collapse with exhaustion by the end of the day. "I've got our sticks ready for roasting. How about you go and get us two hot dogs? Don't worry about the plates or buns right now. We'll get those later. Just get the dogs."

He would have given Jonah one of the sticks to carry but feared the boy might fall and injure himself on the sharp point.

Without a word, Jonah took off like a shot, racing over to the picnic tables. Tanner shook his head and laughed. He'd definitely been smart not to give Jonah one of the pointed sticks.

The camp leaders had set coolers on the tables, filled with various flavors of soda pop and packages of hot dogs, condiments, buns and potato chips. Though the summer sunshine blazed down on them, the cool mountain breeze had forced them to pull on warm jackets. It didn't matter. Everyone laughed and chatted, ignoring the cold.

As Jonah bounced around the tables, Paul's gaze raked the active little boy with repugnance. "That kid's sure a nuisance, isn't he?"

Something bristled inside Tanner. "Not to me."

Paul blinked in surprise. "You really like him?"

"I certainly do." Tanner didn't hesitate to answer, realizing he told the absolute truth. In fact, it irritated him that Paul didn't like Jonah. Besides being incredibly cute, Jonah also had a guileless, winning way about him. Tanner figured it took a crabby disposition for someone not to like the boy.

"Hmm. I like his mother okay, but I'd rather do without her annoying brat," Paul said.

Tanner's hands clenched. He didn't like this man calling Jonah a brat. Not at all. But he was an outsider here and didn't want to start a fight. Instead, he bit his tongue.

"Jonah's not a brat. He's a wonderful little boy. We're lucky to have him and Zoë in our congregation." Blaine Milan spoke from across the campfire where he knelt on one knee as he laid more wood on the flames.

Thank you! Tanner knew there was a good reason he liked Blaine. "I agree. Jonah's smart and lively. He'll make a good man someday."

"I've been thinking about asking Zoë out. On a real date," Paul continued, ignoring Blaine's frown of disapproval.

"That right?" A defensive tingle rose along Tanner's spine. He had no right to tell Zoë whom to date, but he sure didn't want her going out with someone like Paul Carter. The guy seemed to be a playboy. Always on the hunt for another conquest. No commitment. No caring. Tanner wanted to mention his misgivings to Zoë but didn't know how to do so without sounding jealous. Which he wasn't.

Well, maybe a little.

"Dad, I dropped my hot dog in the dirt. And Tim broke my stick." Josh, Paul's nine-year-old son, held out the thin pieces of pine. The boy sniffed, his eyes red from crying.

Tanner noticed the thin shaft of the stick had never been sturdy enough to support a hot dog in the first place. Josh needed help from his dad, but it didn't appear he'd get it anytime soon.

"Go get another stick and leave me alone," Paul snapped, barely sparing his son a glance.

The boy flinched, looking hurt but not surprised by his father's anger, then backed away cautiously.

"You got any more kids?" Tanner asked in casual conversation, his gaze briefly locking with Blaine's as they communicated in a glance their disgust for Paul. But since this was a church function, they had to be nice. They had to be Christian and love everyone. Or at least try.

Tanner was trying very hard. He really was.

"Just these two, thank goodness. They each have different mothers. I like the women fine, but the kids get on my nerves.

They're both clingy, like their moms." Paul jerked his thumb toward his two sons. Without an effective way to cook their food, they'd resorted to eating their hot dogs cold.

Tanner clenched his jaw, resisting the urge to help the boys. They weren't his responsibility, but he couldn't seem to help himself. When Tim grimaced at his raw food, Tanner stood and found two more sturdy sticks. In no time, he had the wood whittled and ready to use.

"Here you go, boys. Now you can cook your hot dogs, but be careful not to fall on the sharp points." He handed the slim branches of pine to the kids.

"Gee, thanks, Tanner!" Josh showed a toothless smile that looked a lot like his dad's.

"Yeah, thanks," Tim chimed in, his voice sounding stunned, as though he couldn't believe someone had actually helped him.

The two boys carried their sticks over to the hot-dog table where Jonah stood laughing at something Billie had said.

"You didn't need to do that. They're old enough to look out for themselves," Paul grumbled.

"No, they're not." Maybe Tanner shouldn't have said that, but he wouldn't take it back.

A flash of anger filled Paul's eyes and he opened his mouth to respond. Tanner didn't give him the chance. He turned and walked to the other side of the fire, biting back an angry retort about rotten parents. He must remain civil on this outing; otherwise, Zoë might hear about it later. Tanner didn't want her upset. She'd entrusted him with her child, and he wouldn't do anything to jeopardize her confidence in him.

To soothe his jangled nerves, Tanner avoided Paul and focused on Jonah. The boy skipped over to the fire. Tanner chuckled. Jonah didn't know how to walk anywhere. He scampered, ran, sprinted, hopped, scurried and dashed. But never walked.

"Here they are." Looking enormously

pleased with himself, Jonah held up two raw hot dogs with his bare hands.

Tanner eyed the dogs, together with Jonah's grimy fingers, and didn't bat an eye. He figured it was his own fault for telling the boy not to worry about plates right now. And the germs should cook off just fine.

Instead, he wrapped an arm around the child's shoulders and helped him thread the meat onto one pointy stick. "If you do it lengthwise like this, your dog won't fall off into the fire. But if you poke the stick into the middle, you'll be more likely to lose your dog."

"Okay." Jonah nodded, soaking up every word Tanner said.

Just like fishing, Tanner realized he could show this boy a lot of things. It felt good to share his knowledge with Jonah, even if it was as simple as how to thread a hot dog onto a stick. In Tanner's mind, this was what fathers were for. Quality time was important, but so was quantity time. The thought of Jonah ending up with a father like Paul left Tanner feeling troubled.

Jonah sat beside Tanner on the log, scooting together as they held their roasters over the flames.

"Not too close. You don't want your dog to burn," Tanner cautioned in a gentle voice.

Jonah moved his stick, responding cheerfully. "When I'm done with this one, I'm gonna have another one and another one. I'm gonna eat a zillion hot dogs today."

Tanner felt the little boy's shoulder brush against his arm and a feeling of protective love overwhelmed him. There was no place on earth he'd rather be right now, except perhaps with Zoë. "A zillion hot dogs? You think your tummy can hold that many?"

Paul hovered nearby, a dark scowl creasing his forehead. No doubt he wished Jonah would leave so he could continue milking Tanner for information about Zoë. Tanner just ignored him.

"Sure! I can eat two all by myself.

Maybe more. Then I'm gonna have ice cream. Mom said today's special, so I can eat anything I want."

Tanner could just imagine the feeling of freedom that permission would give a child, and he couldn't help appreciating Zoë's savvy mothering skills. She was the kind of mother Tanner wanted for his own children.

No, he'd better close the door on that thought. And fast.

"That's right. She did tell me you could eat whatever you wanted today. What's your favorite flavor of ice cream?"

"Chocolate."

"I like strawberry and rocky road." Tanner kept up a steady stream of conversation with the boy, hoping Paul would take the hint and get lost.

By early afternoon, Tanner had been brought forward as the expert on fishing techniques. Blaine Milan roped him into offering a mini-class for all the fathers and sons. It felt good to be wanted and needed by this group of men.

"You're good with the kids. Maybe we can take our sons fishing together sometime," Tom Watson said.

Our sons. Strange how everyone seemed to have accepted Tanner and how easily he'd fallen into the role of Jonah's father. Didn't they all know Zoë was moving back to Portland soon?

"Yeah, that would be fun." It *would* be fun—even if it would probably never happen. Tanner's ears burned, but he couldn't deny he liked the friendship the other men offered. He liked being here with Jonah.

The dads soon spread out around Fleshermann Lake with their sons. Boys of all sizes tossed their fishing lines into the water, laughing and talking so loudly that Tanner doubted they'd catch many trout. But Jonah wasn't disappointed by his lack of fish. He told everyone that would listen about the steelhead he'd caught with Tanner and his mom at Kids' Creek Park in town.

"It was this big." The boy held out his arms in an exaggerated stretch.

"Wow, I never caught a fish that big before," Billie said.

"It's because Tanner uses special bait."

"What is it?"

Jonah's forehead creased in a serious frown. "I can't tell you. It's a secret."

Tanner chuckled. "I think it's okay if you tell Billie."

Jonah looked doubtful. "Really?"

Tanner couldn't resist. "As long as he promises not to tell anyone else."

Billie shook his head, a solemn expression on his face. "I won't tell no one."

"Okay." The two boys crowded close together as Jonah whispered the secret in Billie's ear.

Blaine stood close by, watching the children. "So you gonna tell me this secret of yours?"

Looking at his friend, Tanner realized Blaine really wanted to know. He shrugged but kept his voice low so the little boys wouldn't overhear and think he'd betrayed their confidence. "It's just deli shrimp. No big deal. But it makes the boys feel special to share a secret."

Blaine laughed. "Yeah, I remember when I was their age and having a secret was a lot of fun."

By late afternoon, they reeled in their lines to go back to the camp area. Tanner noticed Josh and Tim fishing alone. Paul sat on the other side of the pond, his heels resting on a tree stump, a baseball cap pulled low across his eyes while he took a nap. Tanner was half tempted to get Blaine and Ted to help him dump Paul in the lake.

Blaine walked past, noticed Tanner's gaze and stopped to chat. "Can you believe that guy?"

Tanner just shook his head. He wasn't big on gossip and didn't want to say something that might ruffle anyone's feathers.

Ted joined them, his round face flushed with sunburn. "I wish he'd get into the spirit of this outing and spend some time with his sons. They're at a critical age, and Tim's been getting into trouble at school.

Paul could do a lot to prevent us from losing those boys when they get older."

Tanner agreed but wasn't about to contribute to the discussion. He didn't have kids of his own and didn't feel like an authority. But he figured an absentee dad had a lot to do with his kids falling into crime and bad behavior. The thought of Jonah becoming a miscreant when he became a teenager caused Tanner to inhale a sharp breath. If only he could do something now to stop that from happening.

Blaine nudged Tanner's arm. "You're not gonna let Paul ask Zoë out, are you?"

Tanner frowned. "It's not my business."

"Why don't you make it your business?" Ted said.

"How?"

Blaine pursed his lips together, as though this was obvious. "Ask her out first. You'd be a fool not to."

"Has she said something about it?" Tanner asked.

"Nope. My wife is good friends with her, but Zoë hasn't said a word to her, either. You're a nice guy, Tanner. The right kind of man to make Zoë happy. She's amazing and you'd be crazy to let some other guy take her."

Hearing his own thoughts verbalized caused Tanner's stomach to clench. "She's leaving for Portland at the end of the summer. I don't want to get involved and then lose her."

"So, ask her not to go."

The two men didn't wait for Tanner's reply before they turned and headed down the narrow path to a different fishing spot. Tanner stared after them, thinking they were both crazy. He couldn't just ask Zoë to give up her career and stay with him in Steelhead. Not when they'd never even talked about dating. And for that matter, if they did get involved, Zoë might want him to quit his job and move to Portland. Tanner wasn't sure he'd agree to something like that, so what made him think Zoë might do it for him? And how could he ask her to leave the job she loved? He wouldn't know unless they at least talked about it. And they were a long way from having that kind of serious conversation.

Later, as Tanner paired up with Jonah in the three-legged race and then the watermelon-eating contest, he had the time of his life. But his thoughts kept drifting back to what Blaine and Ted had said. He'd be crazy to let another man take Zoë. But this wasn't a game. This was life. His life. And it hurt when things went wrong.

By the end of the day, Tanner drove Jonah home. The dusky sunlight glinted off the windshield as the boy fell asleep in the truck. Jonah's golden head fell back against the seat, his mouth open wide as he breathed deeply.

Tanner smiled at the innocent trust of this child, enjoying the quiet murmur of the truck engine after such a busy day.

Back in town, he pulled into the driveway at Zoë's house and carried the sleeping boy inside. As Tanner followed Zoë back to Jonah's room and tucked the little guy into bed, one thought repeated in Tanner's brain. He should never have accompanied Jonah on the father-son outing today. He shouldn't have whittled sticks, cooked hot dogs, chatted with the dads or taught the boys to fish. Because now, Tanner only wanted more.

When she heard Tanner's soft knock on her front door, Zoë hurried to open it wide. She glanced at the clock on the wall, worried by the late hour. Worried Tanner's truck might have broken down along the side of the road or gotten a flat tire.

Now her son was home. He was safe. And she could stop fretting.

After kissing her sleeping child on the forehead, she relaxed. She noticed a smear of ketchup on Jonah's chin and a stain of chocolate on his shirt. "Looks like he had plenty to eat."

Tanner nodded, his angular face covered with deep shadows in the darkened room. "He ate everything in sight."

"Thank you for taking him." She whispered the words so she wouldn't disturb Jonah. She didn't mean to be a worrywart, but she'd never been parted from her son for so long.

"You're welcome."

Zoë walked back to the living room and Tanner followed. She wrapped her sweater around her and spoke in a quiet voice. "Did you two have fun?"

He stared at her bare feet and swallowed twice, as though a lump had formed in his throat. A strong emotion filled his eyes, which she didn't recognize. As though he were fighting himself. "Yes, we had the best time. Thank you for sharing your son with me, Zoë. He's a great kid."

His declaration touched Zoë's heart. Even though Jonah's father had died, the Lord had brought this kind man into her little boy's life.

Into her life.

Taking a deep breath, she released it on a sigh. "No matter how much I try, I can't be both a father and a mother to my son. Your willingness to help means a great deal to both Jonah and me."

Tanner stood close. Too close. And yet,

she didn't have the heart to put more distance between them. A sense of longing pulsed through her veins. She wished they could be closer than just friends.

"Would you like to sit down? Are you hungry?" she asked.

He hesitated, as though he felt conflicted.

"No, it's late. I'd better get going." Tanner's gaze lowered to her lips, then shot over to the door. But he didn't take a step. Didn't move a muscle.

Zoë couldn't read his expression in the dimly lit room. His gaze locked with hers for several pounding moments. Then he looked away, as though fighting himself. He seemed almost desperate to leave. And yet, a part of him seemed to want to stay.

"It is late," she agreed, refusing to make this easier on him. Or herself.

"I'll see you tomorrow." He stepped back, breaking eye contact with her.

"Tomorrow? It's Sunday." She bit down on her bottom lip. She'd invited him to church before and he'd refused.

"Yeah, I know." He stood on her front step, the pale moonlight gleaming off his short dark hair. His amber eyes darkened to coal-black.

"But Jonah and I go to church on Sunday."

"Yep, I know."

"Do you want to go to church with Jonah and me?" She asked the taboo question one more time, refusing to give up on Tanner any more than God would ever give up on her. They still had to work together. She didn't want to upset him and make their jobs any more difficult, and yet, she believed she had a duty to encourage Tanner to return to the Lord.

"We'll see." He swiveled around and walked off into the night, leaving her standing there in confusion.

What did he mean? He hadn't said no. But neither had he said yes.

She folded her arms against the balmy night air, watching as he got into his truck and drove away. As his taillights gleamed red at the first stoplight on the corner, she turned and closed the door.

A flicker of hope speared her heart and she couldn't contain a soft laugh of victory.

He hadn't said no.

Tanner drove himself home, a bead of perspiration breaking out on his forehead. His hands trembled around the steering wheel. He parked his truck and sat there in the dark, staring at the lamppost near the mailboxes of his apartment complex. Against every wish and desire of his heart, against his common sense and best interests, he'd fallen in love with Jonah.

And what about Zoë?

He wasn't sure what he felt for her, though he'd come to care deeply for her. Strong feelings he couldn't explain. Even with Cheryl, he'd never felt like this. So content, yet the feeling was intense and consuming. And frightening.

He had to do something fast to quit thinking about Zoë all the time. To quit longing to be near her. To stop himself from loving her.

Like what?

He raked his fingers through his hair, wondering why he kept fighting the attraction between them. He just couldn't seem to let go and take that leap of faith one more time. But he couldn't ignore the way they seemed to fit each other so perfectly, either.

Over the past few weeks, he and Zoë had visited more and more farmers. Most of them had cooperated and agreed to have a fish screen installed on their property. When someone refused, Tanner stood back and let Zoë explain what the unpleasant options might be. He and Zoë seemed to have found a balance in their working relationship. He could no longer deny that he found her highly capable, professional, intelligent and completely wonderful.

He identified with Jonah in more ways than one. The Jonah from the biblical story, that is. The prophet whom the Lord had called on a mission to the wicked people of Nineveh. Instead, Jonah had run away, trying to hide from the world. But he couldn't hide from God. And somehow, the Lord had found Jonah and called him to repent. It'd taken a trip down into a whale's stomach for Jonah to become humble enough to acquiesce to what God wanted him to do.

So now what? Did Tanner need to be swallowed by a whale before he realized what God wanted from him? He couldn't hide anymore. He had to live in this world. He had to open his heart and make a difference. And he could do that for Zoë and her son.

And maybe for himself, too.

Something had happened to him during the father-son outing. Something he couldn't explain. During the morning devotional, he'd felt a calming influence settle over him. A still, small voice whispered within him that everything would be all right. That he didn't need to keep worrying about his relationship with Zoë. But what did that really mean? He had no answers on how to proceed. She'd move back to Portland and he'd stay here. But that was still weeks away. He had to decide what he was going to do in the here and now.

Blaine Milan had invited Tanner to church on Sunday. The man seemed so comfortable in his own skin and genuine in everything he did. Strong in his faith.

Tanner wanted to emulate that.

Tanner hadn't been to church in ages. And now he couldn't help wondering if he'd missed something. The companionship. The worship of God. The insight into his own needs, desires and failings, which he needed to overcome.

He liked the way he'd felt during the devotional that morning, listening to the simple yet sweet opening prayer offered by a boy not much older than Jonah. And then the short lesson on God's love for all His children and heeding the Holy Spirit. Tanner couldn't explain all the emotions he'd felt today, but he knew he liked them. And he craved more of the same. He felt happy for the first time in a long time. And it was all because of Zoë and Jonah.

Perhaps Zoë was right. Maybe it was time to let go of his indifference toward God. He realized without being told that if he did that he'd also forgive Cheryl for what she'd done. He wouldn't be bitter about losing his parents and grandparents when he was young. And that sounded so appealing. So freeing. He just didn't want to be angry anymore. At anyone.

Hmm. Maybe he ought to take Blaine up on his invitation. Maybe even a gruff fish-and-wildlife specialist like him deserved a second chance with the Lord.

Chapter Ten

"Billie, your mom's here," Zoë called toward the back of her house as she opened the front door.

Debbie stood on the porch step wearing a pair of capris and sandals, her cheeks flushed with color as she shifted her baby on her hip. Mindy, her toddler, clung to her other hand. "Hi, Zoë. Was Billie any trouble this afternoon?"

"Of course not. The boys play so quietly together I have to check on them frequently just to see what they might be up to." She picked up Mindy and stepped back to let Debbie inside.

"I know what you mean. Sometimes

quietness is a sign of disaster. I made the mistake of ignoring Mindy once when she was playing too quietly and discovered she'd plugged the bathroom sink and flooded the bathroom with water."

Zoë cringed with sympathy. "Oh, no! That would not be fun."

Debbie set the baby on the floor before she plopped down into a soft chair. Making happy bubbling sounds, the infant immediately crawled across the Berber carpet and pulled himself up against the sofa. Zoë set Mindy on her feet and the girl plopped down beside a basket of toys.

"Would you like something to drink?" Zoë offered.

"I'd love a glass of water. It's hot outside today."

Zoë retrieved a glass before filling it with ice and chilled water from the fridge. She returned to the living room and handed the glass to Debbie. "Did you get your shopping done?"

"Yep." Debbie took several swallows before lowering the glass.

They chatted for several minutes, in no hurry to chase down the boys.

"You'll never guess who I saw downtown in the grocery store." Debbie took another sip from her glass.

"Who?"

"Tanner Bohlman."

"Oh?" Every muscle in Zoë's body tightened, but she tried not to show her reaction.

Debbie's shrewd gaze rested on Zoë like a ten-ton sledge. "Are you gonna tell me what's going on between you two?"

Zoë shifted nervously in her chair. "What do you mean?"

"Come on. I see the way you two look at each other."

"Nothing's going on. We work together, nothing more."

"Yeah, right. I have eyes in my head. You both light up like the Fourth of July every time you see each other. He asked me about you today."

"He did?"

"Yes, he asked if you were watching Billie for me. I told him you were. I also told him he should call and ask you out."

Zoë gasped. "No, tell me you didn't do that."

Debbie laughed. "No, I didn't, but I sure wanted to. You two seem made for each other."

Zoë scoffed, trying not to feel nervous about this conversation. "Tanner and I work together—that's all."

"You sure it isn't something more? He did take Jonah on the father-son outing, after all."

"He was just being kind. There's nothing to it. At least not for him. He's struggling with his own problems and needs to figure them out by himself."

"You're talking about Cheryl."

Zoë froze. "How do you know about Cheryl?"

The chair creaked as Debbie sat forward. She reached to help balance the toddler as the little girl held on to the edge of the coffee table and crossed the carpet. "You forget I've lived here all my life. This is a small town and people talk. I remember when Cheryl broke Tanner's heart. His best friend came to visit just weeks before their wedding and that was that."

Though she didn't like gossip, Zoë had to ask. "What happened between them?"

Debbie lifted one shoulder. "Cheryl moved to Boise and married the other guy. Apparently, Tanner took it real hard. Not only did he lose the woman he loved just before their wedding, but he also lost his best friend."

Zoë bit back a gasp. "His best friend?"

"Correction. His ex-best friend."

"Oh, no."

"Oh, yes."

Zoë bit her bottom lip, her heart aching for Tanner's loss. "Poor Tanner."

"So, have you told him you're interested in him yet?"

Confusion fogged Zoë's mind. "Of course not. I don't know what you mean."

"It's obvious, honey. You like him. A lot. Why not tell him? Blaine is friends with him. Believe me, my hubby was furious when he heard what Cheryl had done. We'd love to see Tanner happily settled with someone who deserves him. And you'd be great together. You have so much in common and he obviously loves Jonah. He's tall and handsome and you're so gorgeous. He's a great catch and you'd make a cute couple."

Zoë had heard enough. Shaking her head, she stood. "Maybe for someone else. I've got my hands full with my own life. I don't need any more complications. Besides, I'm moving back to Portland soon."

"You ought to think about staying here."

"No, my job is there." She didn't add that Tanner had trust issues. She didn't want to immerse herself and Jonah in that kind of trouble. Tanner would have to reconcile his problems on his own terms. Something like this couldn't be rushed. And Zoë didn't want herself or Jonah to be a casualty in the process.

"Can't you get another job here?"

Zoë snorted. "In this economy?"

"Yeah, it'd probably be the same problem if Tanner moved to Portland. I can see you don't want to talk about it. But if you ever change your mind, I'm willing to listen." Debbie picked up the baby, grabbed her toddler's hand and stood before calling for Billie again.

After they'd left, Zoë sat on the sofa in her living room and hugged a tasseled pillow to her chest. Her gaze was fixed on the TV, but she didn't see the evening news or follow any of the dialogue. Her mind kept traveling back over what Debbie had said.

Tanner was a great catch and she had strong feelings for him, but she had to accept the truth that he wasn't the man for her. She needed someone who was calm, settled and loved the Lord as much as she did. Someone from Portland. So why did she keep perusing the job listings for this area? And why did she entertain thoughts of staying in Steelhead instead of returning to Oregon?

Yes, Tanner was good at his job, handsome, smart and funny. But he wasn't what a widow with a young son to raise needed in her life. No, not at all.

Zoë waded into the stream. Even through her rubber knee-high waders, she felt the warm temperature of the water swirling about her ankles. Not crisp and cold, like a healthy creek ought to be.

Tall tree trunks, grayed by death and devoid of leaves, lined the meandering flow of Hansen Creek. A clutter of dried sticks and vegetation clung to the yellowed rocks and sloping banks. There was no life whatsoever showing within the riparian area. Looking up, she gazed at the caustic water. It ran clear, but it couldn't be healthy.

Something had killed this creek. No doubt that something was the now-defunct cobalt and copper mine sitting a scant mile above them high in the Bingham Mountains.

Two hours earlier, Tanner had taken Zoë to view the five million tons of waste-rock piles at the abandoned mine. She'd never worked on a mine contamination cleanup before, but she knew what it meant to the environment. Each time a thunderstorm or snowmelt hit the area, soils filled with arsenic, zinc, cobalt and copper washed down the mountain, killing every living thing it came into contact with.

Cautious not to lose her footing on the slick rocks, she straddled the creek and leaned down to dip a glass vial into the water to take another sample. She snapped the lid onto the vial, then scrawled a few notes on the label. Her rubber gloves gave her a better grip on the slippery vials. For the umpteenth time since she'd first dipped her hands into the water, she scratched her right wrist, then her lower arm. Maybe she'd been bitten by mosquitoes.

"How's it going?" Tanner called nearby from shore.

Wearing his green Forest Service uniform, he rested his hands on his lean hips. The wind flicked his dark hair across his high forehead, giving him a disheveled, masculine appearance.

As usual, he'd driven her up here, describing the condition of the tributary and surrounding area. So far, their conversation had been completely sterile. Only once had Tanner asked how Jonah was doing. That was it. No mention of the father-son outing. No discussion about the wonderful time the boys had together. No appearance at church yet.

"Good. Almost done," she said.

She scratched again, surprised to find a pinkish rash covering her wrist. Almost like an allergic reaction to something. Maybe the new lotion she'd worn that morning. Or perhaps she'd brushed against a poisonous plant as she'd hiked along the waterway. Hmm. Very odd.

Shrugging it off, she placed the samples inside the hip bag she wore draped sideways across her body, then moved farther downstream to the confluence where Hansen Creek joined with Clear Creek. She waded out into the middle of the stream. The swifter current beat against her calves, threatening to knock her over if she wasn't careful.

Sloshing over to the shore, she dipped a last vial into the bluish mud of the stream-bed. In a normal riparian area, this soil should be black and rich with nutrients.

"You getting the samples you need?" Tanner stood nearby, his cheeks and nose showing a hint of sunburn.

She faced him. "Yes. You know, I've been thinking. You mentioned that the lower seven miles of Bingham River has dried up due to water diversion by irrigators. There isn't enough water for the fish to swim up or down the river, so they can't get through to the tributaries and reach their spawning beds. You also said the farmers and ranchers don't need all the water they've been taking out for irrigation."

Tanner nodded. "That's correct. Right now, the farmers take out too much."

She shifted her weight, continuing with her idea. "So, what if we ask the farmers to cut their water use in half for three days and nights in a row? That short a time shouldn't cause them any duress. We could coordinate the dates with them so we're all on the same schedule and see if it might make a difference in the water level of the river."

Tanner stared at Zoë. Why hadn't he thought of this? "You know, that just might work. It certainly couldn't hurt. I'll bet the Fish and Wildlife Service would help us with the project."

Her sun-kissed nose crinkled with her smile. "And we could time it for when the salmon are ready to swim upriver. Three days would give them all the time they need to go up and for the smaller fish to come down on their journey to the ocean."

Yes! The more he thought about this idea, the more he liked it. He smiled wide, barely able to contain his enthusiasm. "Zoë, I think it just might work. You know that fish trap we have at the mouth of Bingham River? We could hold the fish there until the water conditions are right, then open it to let the fish come upstream. We would know very soon if it was working. It's a cooperative gesture that would involve a lot of different players, but I don't know many farmers who would refuse to help for such a short time."

"Well, you taught me that compromise and cooperation get the job done better than threats."

He gave her a quizzical frown. "I taught you that?"

"Uh-huh. Among other things." Her face lit up in a teasing smile.

"What other things?"

She just laughed but didn't say anything further.

For the next thirty minutes, they discussed plans for their new project. How to get word out to all the farmers. Who should be involved in the endeavor. The best time for the experiment to take place so that it allowed the most fish to move up and down the river. How they might track and determine their rate of success.

Tanner took a cleansing breath. "I'll call for a meeting first thing next week."

"Good. We'll need to get moving quickly. We've got just enough time to set it all up before the fish need to start their trek upstream."

Filled with expectations, he waited while Zoë labeled her last sample and tucked it inside her bag with the others.

When she climbed out of the water, she rubbed both her wrists. "I've got to get these gloves off. My hands and arms are itching like crazy."

Tanner held her elbow as she climbed over the rocks. While she pulled off her gloves, he handed her a dry towel so she could mop off the water. She sat on the ground near her dry socks and hiking boots and gasped.

"Look at this!" She pointed at her gloves, then her hip waders.

Tanner was surprised to see small holes dotting each rubber boot. "What on earth do you think caused it?"

"I have no idea. The holes weren't there

when I put my boots on several hours ago. It looks like little bugs have eaten their way through my waders."

"Do you think the high concentration of copper could have done this?"

"It's hard to know for sure. It's ironic that there's so much focus on nuclear waste when we're leaving tons of mine tailings in our mountains to contaminate our streams. The tailings problem will be here forever."

Tanner grasped the toe of one wader and tugged while Zoë pushed the boot off. She'd stuffed the pant legs of her blue jeans down into the waders to keep them dry. Her gaze lifted to Tanner's face. "I'm just thankful no water invaded my boots."

"Me, too." He gazed at her hands with misgivings. The rash covered every inch of her fingers and wrists.

"I think this is a chemical burn." She rubbed her open palms, careful not to scratch and make the wounds worse.

Tanner knelt beside her, concerned by

her discomfort. "What would have caused this?"

They both turned to stare at the creek. The trickling sound of the stream moving across the rocks appeared harmless and soothing to the ear. At first glance, nothing seemed out of the ordinary, except the absence of plant life.

"You didn't happen to notice any fish or frogs swimming in the stream, did you?" Tanner asked.

Zoë shook her head. "Not even a single bug or fly. Something's seriously wrong here, Tanner. Something bad."

He nodded. "Yeah, wait right here. I'll get the first-aid kit."

He jogged toward the green Forest Service truck parked two hundred yards away, conscious of her gaze following him. By the time he returned carrying a case of bottled water, she had her socks and boots back on her feet.

"Whatever you were working in needs to be rinsed off right now," he said.

Nodding at his common sense, she let

him pop the lids of each bottle and drain the fresh water over her arms. He then knelt beside her and wrapped a clean orange towel around each of her hands.

She laughed. "I feel like I'm wearing two fat jack-o'-lanterns. I can't wait to get these samples back to my lab."

He didn't look up from his work, trying to be infinitely gentle as he spread the cream over her skin. "We're going to the hospital first."

Because her hands were wrapped up, he helped her stand, then gathered up the other damp towels and her bags.

Back in the truck, he turned onto the main road and headed down the mountain. An urgency built within him to get her back to town. The burns on her hands could be serious, and he wasn't about to let them linger without medical care.

He tried to tell himself his concern was just because she was a coworker and he was responsible for her. But deep inside, he knew it was much more than that. He just refused to acknowledge it right now. And he possibly never would.

Chapter Eleven

Thirty-five minutes later, Zoë was grateful for Tanner's help. By the time they pulled into the emergency parking lot of the hospital in town, her hands burned like fire, the rash a bright, angry red.

Tanner accompanied her inside where he placed her in a chair, then hurried over to the reception desk. "We need a doctor right now, please."

At least he was polite about it.

"What seems to be the problem, sir?"

He quickly explained. "She's in a lot of pain."

Very interesting, considering Zoë hadn't told him this. But Tanner always seemed in tune with what she was thinking. As he leaned his arms against the front counter, he shifted his weight impatiently. And in a rush, his urgency reminded her that she wasn't alone. For the first time in years, she had someone else looking out for her. And it felt good.

The receptionist handed Tanner a clipboard to take down her information. Tucking the clipboard beneath his arm, he returned to Zoë. His gaze scanned her face, as though searching for signs of distress. She'd never seen Tanner like this before. So concerned. So agitated and worried. As if he really cared.

Zoë reached for her purse, but Tanner slipped it away. Holding the pen and clipboard in his fingers, he wrote fast, his handwriting almost illegible as she dictated to him. It felt good to have Tanner here. His presence made her feel protected and safe.

"Remind me to never go kayaking in that tributary." She tried to laugh, but the pain in her hands caused her to grimace instead.

He tilted his head, his hand never ceasing its movement as he wrote out her address, phone number and employment information. "You know how to kayak?"

She lifted one shoulder and smiled as happy memories from long ago washed through her mind. "Very well. My husband and I used to kayak the American River all the time, before I had Jonah. But I haven't been since—"

The words caught in her throat. A rush of loneliness caused her to inhale a sharp breath.

"Since your husband died," Tanner finished for her, glancing at her face.

She nodded, a deluge of tears pressing against the back of her eyes. Recognizing that she was feeling especially vulnerable right now, she refused to give in to her sudden emotions. Instead, she gazed at the crisp seams along the sleeves of his Forest Service shirt.

"How'd you like to go again?" he asked,

slapping the pen on top of the clipboard as he reached to help her stand.

Her gaze met his. "What do you mean?"

He flashed that dazzling, lopsided smile of his. "With me. I'd like to take you kayaking. I still need to give you a tour of Whisper Creek. I guarantee that water won't burn your hands. It's pure and clean. And what better way to see it than to go kayaking? It has some amazing white water, but not too swift. Just what you need to get back into the groove of the sport."

"I'd like that very much."

As Zoë walked across the foyer, an orderly scurried over with a wheelchair and insisted she sit down. A sudden lump formed in her chest and she tried to swallow. For some crazy reason, Tanner's invitation lit her up from the inside. Then she remembered this was just business. Nothing more.

He glanced down at the tips of her swollen fingers poking out of the towels. They weren't pretty right now. No, they were inflamed and as red as beets.

"I'm so sorry about this," he said.

Her heart felt as though it plunged downward toward her toes, wishing things could be different between them but knowing it was futile. "I know. I'll be okay."

The orderly pushed Zoë toward the hallway with Tanner walking close beside her.

"When do you want to go kayaking?" he asked.

"Soon."

His gaze caressed her reddened wrists, his eyes filled with compassion. "I can schedule the trip once you're well enough."

"You name the day and time and I'll be ready. I can make arrangements for Debbie Milan to watch Jonah next week."

"That might be too soon."

"Not for me."

He licked his bottom lip, as though he regretted the suggestion. They could just drive up. They didn't need to kayak the river. She wouldn't force him, but she did look forward to the trip.

"I was thinking we should go in a few weeks. I'll call you at home later to confirm the date and time," he said.

"Do you have my home number?"

He reached into his pants pocket and pulled out a crumpled piece of paper. As he unfolded it, she recognized the same note she'd written her name and cell-phone number on that crazy day when Jonah had crashed their shopping cart into Tanner's truck.

So. He hadn't thrown it away. He still had it with him. Maybe he wasn't as remote about his feelings for her, after all.

"I've got it right here." Tanner gave her a sheepish smile as the orderly pushed her inside an examination room.

Zoë didn't say a word. She didn't have to. Tanner would call her later. She knew it. He wouldn't dare cancel on her. She was an invalid right now. And if a chemical burn was what it took to get Tanner to lower some of his barriers, maybe it had been worth it.

* * *

Tanner stayed at the hospital and drove Zoë home later that evening.

"I'm sorry about your hands," he said for the umpteenth time.

"It wasn't your fault. And you didn't need to stay with me all this time. I could have found my own ride home."

And yet, he still felt responsible. "Nonsense. It's the least I could do. I should have taken the samples instead of you. I knew that creek was bad. I should have put you in a hazmat suit before letting you into that water."

She reached across the expanse of the truck cab and touched his arm with her bandaged fingertips. "We didn't know it was severe, Tanner. The doctor said I should be fine within a week or two."

Tanner kept his eyes on the road. Her reassuring words washed over him like a soothing caress, but he still felt rotten about what had happened. He hated seeing her suffer even the slightest bit. His stomach clenched when he thought of how serious the damage to her hands might have been. It wasn't anyone's fault except the mine owners', but he still felt responsible for her.

"Is Jonah at home now?" she asked.

"No, I got hold of the Milans, as you suggested. I spoke to Blaine. They're keeping Jonah at their place overnight. Debbie will feed him dinner and give you time to rest your hands. They'll get him ready and bring him to church tomorrow morning, too."

Zoë nodded. "Dear Debbie and Blaine."

"Nice folks."

"Yes, they are. Do you have a best friend?" she asked.

He tightened his fingers around the steering wheel, wishing she hadn't brought that up. "I did once."

"But no more?"

A rush of memories filled his mind. Of him and Dave clowning around on the high school football team. Double-dating the homecoming queen and first runner-up. Hanging out at the local burger joint after school when they should have been home studying. Rooming together at Idaho State University in Pocatello. All the times they'd watched each other's back. And then the hurtful betrayal.

"No, we're not friends anymore," he murmured.

"Why not?"

"He stole Cheryl, my fiancée." There, he'd said the words out loud. For the first time since it'd happened.

"Ouch," she whispered. "I'm sure that hurt."

"It did." He glanced at Zoë, feeling ugly inside.

"Did they get married?"

An icy fist clutched his heart. "Yes. I think they're expecting their first child now."

Dave had stolen the life Tanner planned for himself. He'd thought that finally he was going to have a family of his own. Someone to love. A place of belonging. A permanent home.

He'd been wrong.

"Then they're still happy together?" Zoë said.

Tanner nodded, not daring to speak right now. Dave and Cheryl's happiness was a constant reminder that it should have been him.

"I'm sorry they hurt you."

He glanced at Zoë and caught the deep sympathy in her eyes.

"I keep going over what happened in my mind, trying to figure out what I did wrong," he confessed.

"You did nothing wrong, Tanner. There's no way to really explain why we fall in love with one special person. It happens. And then when we marry them, we have to lock our hearts and give only our spouse the key. I'm glad Cheryl didn't marry you and hurt you later on."

She gave him a soft smile, and somehow he didn't feel quite as angry anymore. In fact, with Zoë here, the loss seemed to evaporate like dew beneath the summer sun. It just wasn't there.

He shrugged. "They were in love and I wish them well."

She reached over and nudged his arm with one bandaged hand. "Do you really mean that?"

He paused for several heartbeats, feeling the warm consolation of her touch. He listened to the sound of the truck engine as the tires sped across the gravel road leading up to Zoë's house. As he searched his deepest feelings, he listened to his inner voice to discover the truth. "Yes. I'm glad we found out early, before I married Cheryl and we ended up divorced. I wouldn't want to marry a woman who loved someone else."

Zoë smiled. "I know it must have been very hard on you at the time, but I'm glad Cheryl and Dave found each other, too."

He'd never looked at it that way. Yes, he'd been hurt when Cheryl had told him she didn't really love him. That she'd fallen for Dave and planned to marry him. But Tanner had been so wrapped up in his own hurt that he hadn't stopped to think about her happiness. And now he realized that if he'd really loved Cheryl the way a man should love a woman, he would have put her joy above his own without even trying.

In Zoë's driveway, Tanner killed the motor and hurried to help her out of the truck. He held her arm until they were inside the house where he caught the faint aroma of cinnamon and apples. A homemade pie with fluted edges sat on the kitchen table along with a toy train.

"I made that for you." Zoë nodded at the table.

He swallowed hard. "The train?"

She laughed at his humor. "No, silly. The pie."

"You did?"

"Uh-huh. As a way of saying thank-you for all you've done for Jonah."

He didn't need to ask why. Obviously, she'd listened when he'd revealed his fond memories of his grandmother's homemade pie. And like it or not, he couldn't resist Zoë's offering. In fact, the gesture squeezed his heart with such a longing for family and home that it almost hurt.

Chapter Twelve

Standing in her kitchen, Zoë's gaze met and locked with Tanner's for several pounding moments. Neither one spoke, and the air filled with a sizzle of expectancy and hope.

He looked away first, taking a step back as he slid his hands into his pants pockets. "Is there anything you need before I get going? I know it can be rough without the full use of your hands."

"No, I'll be fine. With the meds they gave me, I have no pain at all. The burns will heal quickly enough."

Why hadn't she said yes? *I need your help. I need you to stay and help me fix something for dinner and turn on the TV and cuddle up on the couch and watch an old movie with me. I need you, Tanner. I need your love.*

Zoë shook her head, wondering where all these sentimental thoughts had come from. Allowing herself to think this way would only make leaving for Portland that much harder.

"Okay, I'd better get going, then." He turned toward the door.

"Wait!" She hurried over to the table and picked up the pie. Not an easy achievement with her bandaged hands. Maybe she needed his help more than she realized. Stepping close, she gave him the pie. He held it in his hands, a quiet barrier between them.

Zoë stayed close for several seconds, knowing she was being forward. Knowing she was jostling him out of his sad comfort zone. She told herself it was just because she'd hurt her hands today. But somehow, she knew her feelings went deeper than that. In spite of her desire not to, she was falling for this man. She just hoped and prayed it didn't hurt too much when she hit the ground. And for the umpteenth time, she wished she didn't have to return to Portland in the fall.

"Thanks, Zoë. I appreciate it." His voice sounded low and husky with emotion. Maybe she'd gotten through to him after all. Maybe—

"I've got to go now."

Okay, maybe not.

He gave her that quirky smile of his that told her he was beyond uncomfortable.

"Will we see you at church tomorrow?" We, as in her and Jonah. "Blaine will be there and the other dads you met on the father-son outing," she hurried to add.

He stiffened and she immediately regretted asking the question.

"We'll see."

As he stepped outside, the screen door clapped closed and she watched him saunter over to his truck. The warm evening air gathered around her, smelling of sweet honeysuckle. The setting sun had just started to disappear beyond the western mountains.

The slamming of his truck door jarred her back to reality.

"Great, Zoë. Way to throw yourself at the poor guy," she scolded.

She closed the front door, not expecting to see Tanner at church tomorrow or ever.

But she was wrong.

Zoë was already sitting in a back pew the next morning when Debbie and Blaine entered the chapel with Billie, Jonah and the other Milan children.

"Mom! Are you okay?" Her son hugged her tight, gazing at her bandaged hands as if they were an entire body cast.

She kissed his face. "Of course, sweetheart. Did you have fun on your sleepover?"

"Uh-huh." He slid across the row and plopped down with Billie, waiting obediently for the meeting to start.

Debbie shifted her toddler in her arms

and sat next to Zoë. "Are you really all right?"

"Yes, really. Just some mild burns that will heal soon."

And then Zoë looked up and saw Tanner Bohlman standing in the doorway. A warm, tingly feeling buzzed through her arms and legs. Like the anticipation of Christmas morning, only ten times better.

"Hi, Tanner. It's good to see you here." Blaine greeted the other man with a handshake. "Why don't you sit with us?"

Wow! If Zoë thought Tanner had been handsome in his Forest Service uniform, she could hardly take her eyes off him in his dark pin-striped suit. Gone were his scuffed work boots, replaced by shiny black wing-tip shoes. His lean cheeks showed that he'd shaved that morning, and he smelled faintly of spicy aftershave.

Debbie nudged her with a knowing smile. Without being asked, the woman stood and stepped across Zoë so she could sit on the opposite side. Her intention was obvious. She was making room for Tanner to sit next to Zoë.

"Hi, Tanner!" Jonah waved, his face beaming.

Tanner nodded, then his gaze locked with Zoë's. "Is it all right if I sit here?"

"Of course." She made a pretense of shifting down the bench to give him more room.

Rather than stumble across everyone, Blaine went around to the opposite side and sat next to the little boys, bringing the baby's carrier with him. Zoë knew he'd make sure the children behaved during the service. It felt good to be sitting with friends and family.

It felt good to be sitting beside Tanner.

"I'm so glad you're here," she said. And she meant it with every beat of her heart.

He smiled but didn't say a word.

Tanner wiped his brow and hoped he hadn't just made a big mistake by showing up at church today. He didn't want to give Zoë the wrong impression. They were coworkers and friends. That was all. Nothing more. And yet, he'd become so hungry for companionship—*her* companionship—that he couldn't resist being here. If only he didn't feel so comfortable around her and Jonah. If only he didn't care about them.

But he did.

He listened intently to the message, absorbing every word. Remembering the scriptures and lessons his grandparents had taught him so long ago. It all came whooshing back, so nice and familiar. Like long-lost friends he'd learned to live without but never could quite forget.

Later in Sunday school class, Blaine introduced him to everyone. At first, he felt alone in a deep sea of unfamiliar faces. But then he recognized several of the dads. Everyone was so welcoming that he soon felt right at home.

Except with Paul. When Tanner sat beside Zoë, Paul glared daggers at both of them. Tanner did his best to ignore the other man but couldn't help saying something about it to Zoë.

"I think he's feeling territorial."

At her questioning glance, Tanner nodded toward Paul, who turned around with a huff and sat stiffly in his seat.

Her lips tightened. "As far as I'm concerned, he has no territory."

"You sure about that? He let me know on the father-son outing that he has plans to ask you out. Maybe I shouldn't—"

"I'm positive. He's called and asked me out several times since then. I've tried to make it clear I'm not interested, but the guy won't take no for an answer. Maybe with you here, he'll leave me alone for once." She gave a shudder of repugnance, then shook her head in exasperation.

Tanner's stomach turned several cartwheels. Even though he had no right, he'd been feeling a bit jealous. Now he felt amazingly relieved. "Good. He's not the man for you."

"Is that so?"

He didn't answer. She gave him a curious look, her blue eyes crinkled in surprise, but she didn't comment further. Thank goodness. If she pressed the issue, he wasn't sure how he'd explain himself.

Later, he learned that Zoë normally played the piano for the children during singing time. With her fingers wrapped up like little mummies, she couldn't do it today. Several people remarked about her injury, but she downplayed it all.

"It was Tanner's quick thinking that made it better," she insisted. "He rinsed my hands with fresh water."

Though he'd done very little, Tanner couldn't help feeling pleased by her praise. He felt as if they were a team.

He leaned close and whispered in her ear, "I didn't know you played the piano."

She nodded, and he was once again surprised by her many talents. Was there anything this woman couldn't do? He kept finding more and more to like about her every day.

"By the way, your apple pie was delicious," he told her.

A wide smile lit up her sparkling blue eyes. "I'm glad. Did you eat it all last night or save some for today?"

He chuckled, enjoying her sense of humor. "I was so hungry when I got home that I ate it all. I should have shared it with you."

But he'd been so dazed that he hadn't thought about staying with her a little bit longer. He'd felt nervous and fearful of his own feelings and had gotten away from her as fast as he could. So he could think clearly.

It hadn't helped. He was as confused by his feelings for this woman as ever.

"There will be other pies," she promised, resting her bandaged hands in her lap.

He glanced at her dainty, flowered dress, amazed by her transformation. At work, she wore hip waders and tromped through muddy creekbeds. Then she'd change into some feminine concoction that made his senses roar into awareness. She had so many different facets to her and he valued every one.

She gazed serenely up at the front of the class, listening intently to the teacher. He took a moment to admire her delicate profile and flawless skin.

"Are we still going kayaking?" she whispered for his ears alone.

"Yes, of course we are. I've already scheduled it for several weeks from now."

A woman sitting in the row directly in front of them tossed a scolding frown his way. He clamped his mouth closed, thinking he should shut up and pay attention.

"Good." Zoë ducked her head on the pretense of smoothing a wrinkle of fabric over her left thigh.

He stared at her sleek calves and high heels, then slumped down a bit in his chair so he could come more level with her head. Maybe he shouldn't have suggested the kayaking trip. He'd had a moment of weakness because her hands had been injured. Because he'd wanted to protect her and make her happy. Now he'd put his own heart at risk. He could fall in love with this woman so easily. He just hoped it wasn't too late already.

"When can you meet to discuss the water-irrigation project?" He spoke as quietly as he could.

She took a deep inhale and let it go, her voice a low caress. "Tomorrow."

"I can stop by your office in the morning."

"That sounds fine."

The woman in front of them flounced around and gave them another sober glare, this time with a huffy sigh added. Zoë choked back a laugh. Like a naughty girl chastised by her mother, yet not repentant in the least.

"You're gonna get us into trouble," he warned, waggling his eyebrows at her.

She didn't respond, but her smile remained.

Yep, he was hooked. He could no longer deny he had serious feelings for this woman. But what should he do about those feelings? His dilemma was getting worse every day.

After her Sunday meetings ended, Zoë stood in the front foyer waiting to speak with Tanner before going home. Jonah should be getting out of his class soon. Maybe she'd invite Tanner to—

"Hi, Zoë."

She turned with a smile and faced...Paul Carter. Her smile dropped like a stone and her stomach gave a violent twist. She'd hoped to avoid him today.

"Hi, Paul." She didn't smile as she took two steps back.

He followed, closing the distance between them, reaching out to clasp her upper arm as he showed his toothy grin. "I'm glad we have a moment to speak alone. I finally understand why you've been turning me down every time I ask you out."

She blinked, shrugging his hand off her arm. His heavy cologne assailed her nostrils and she tried to hold her breath. "You do?"

"Yeah, Blaine Milan told me you'll be moving back to Portland soon. I want to reassure you that isn't a problem for me."

She took a sideways step but found her path blocked by a potted tree. A spindly branch and leaves batted her in the face, so she held up her hand for protection. "And why is that?"

"I'm relatively set financially, you know. I can live anywhere I choose. And I've always wanted to visit Portland."

A blaze of horror shot up her spine. "No, that won't work. Not at all."

His grin widened. "I know you've been worried about getting involved with me when you won't be staying in town. But now there's nothing to keep us apart. I can come with you."

"Oh, Paul. No. I'm not interested. I've already told you that a dozen times."

"But I figured it was just because you'll be leaving soon. It's so like you to want to spare my feelings. But seriously, we have no obstacles in our way now."

She gritted her teeth, her mind racing with a rush of words she longed to say but didn't dare utter inside the church. Why could this man not get this through his brain? He had her cornered. Literally. Short of pushing against his chest and being extremely rude, she had very few options left.

Glancing to her left, she saw Millie Archer standing near the door chatting with Sandy Gardner. They each smiled and cast knowing glances in her direction. Zoë didn't want to cause a scene, but neither did she want everyone believing she was romantically involved with this horrible man. A feeling of pure panic clawed at her throat. If Paul didn't give her some space soon, she'd be forced to—

"Ahem, excuse me, Paul."

Zoë peered over Paul's shoulder. Tanner stood there, a forced smile curving his lips. His eyes had darkened to narrowed black points.

Paul turned to look at Tanner, and Zoë didn't hesitate to flee. She slid past the two men, standing just behind Tanner. Without thinking, she reached out and clutched the lower edge of Tanner's sleeve and held on tight. Dizzying relief flooded her entire body. She was not letting go of him until she was far away from Paul.

"Tanner, I was speaking to Zoë." Paul's smile faded to an irritated sneer.

"Yes, I couldn't help overhearing. And I thought you'd like to know why she's continued to turn you down." With Zoë clinging to Tanner's sleeve, the answer probably seemed pretty clear. Zoë was glad that Tanner hadn't actually lied to Paul, but she couldn't claim she minded if his actions made Paul jump to some mistaken conclusions.

Millie and Sandy arched their necks, listening to every word. Paul's pallid face reddened with embarrassment as he cast a glance their way. No doubt his ego didn't take kindly to this humiliation.

"Zoë wanted to spare your feelings,"

Tanner continued. "I'm sure you understand."

"Well, if she's already going with you, I understand. There's plenty of other fish in the sea for me." The hazy look in Paul's eyes indicated he didn't understand a thing, but he had no other option than to politely withdraw. Under the circumstances, Tanner had been very kind to give Paul a graceful way out of this ugly situation.

Tanner reached up and clapped the man on the shoulder in a friendly gesture, then scooped his arm around Zoë's back. Applying slight pressure with his arm, he whisked her down the hall with him. The cry of freedom thrummed within her veins and she didn't resist.

As she walked briskly beside Tanner, she glanced back, catching Paul's annoyed expression. Sandy and Millie tried to engage the man in conversation, but Paul brushed past them without a word and headed outside.

Zoë inwardly groaned. No doubt news

of what Tanner had done would spread throughout the congregation. People would believe she was romantically involved with him. Still, it was a small price to pay if it meant she could rid herself of Paul's unwanted attention.

"I hope I did the right thing. I could see you were in a tight spot." Tanner spoke low for her ears alone as they stopped in front of Jonah's classroom door.

"Oh, yes. Thank you for saving me." She breathed a sigh of relief.

"You're very welcome."

As she looked up into his smiling eyes, she felt overwhelmed by appreciation. Giddy happiness washed through her and she didn't think before she made her next request. "I've got a roast and potatoes simmering in the slow cooker at home. Would you like to join Jonah and me for dinner?"

She'd forgotten her promise not to invite him over again. He needed to make the next move. But she couldn't seem to help herself.

He licked his bottom lip and shifted his

weight. In his amber eyes, she saw a flash of acceptance, but then it was gone. So fast she thought she'd imagined it.

"Sorry, but I can't, Zoë. I just can't."

All right, she'd learned her lesson a second time. The man wasn't interested in her. And yet, she got so many funny vibes from him. A look, a smile, a hesitancy that told her he wanted to be more than friends.

So did she.

As Jonah's class got out and a wriggling bunch of six-year-olds flooded the hallway, Zoë waited for Jonah.

"Tanner!" The boy ran toward the tall man, who dropped to one knee and opened his arms wide for a hug.

Something warm and tight churned within Zoë's chest. Her son loved this man. But she couldn't pursue Tanner. It wouldn't be fair. Because being together would require Tanner to give up his job and move to Portland, or for Zoë to resign her position instead. As much as Zoë and Jonah loved the quaint charm of Steelhead, Zoë couldn't stay here indefinitely. The security of her employment was more important than love.

Wasn't it?

Tanner stood and waved at her. "See you tomorrow."

"Yeah, tomorrow." An ache settled in the pit of her stomach. She no longer looked forward to their meetings. Because they were a constant reminder of what she couldn't have.

Chapter Thirteen

Over the next couple of weeks, Zoë spent hours with Tanner planning their river-irrigation project. While Jonah colored or played with his toys around her desk, she worked late, calling each of the local farmers and ranchers to ask them to participate. She then followed up with a letter. A series of meetings were held. Everyone was notified of the dates when they should reduce their usage of river water. Three days and nights. That's all they needed to make this project work.

She hoped.

Tanner enlisted the help of the State Fish and Game Department as well as other agencies. And the first day of the event, they worked tirelessly to lay white plastic, weighted down by rocks, across a long stretch of the nearly dry riverbed. To document their success or failure, they'd set up video cameras along the embankment. Floodlights would be turned on at night to allow them to see any fish moving through the stream channel. A lot of resources had gone into this venture. Even the media had been invited to this event. If it failed, Zoë wouldn't need to worry about returning to Portland. She would be more than disappointed.

She could lose her job.

Zoë sat next to Tanner beside the dry streambed, both of them wolfing down cheeseburgers. Although it was late afternoon, they'd both been so busy that they'd forgotten to eat lunch until now.

"Do you think this will work?" She poked a French fry into her mouth, unable to disguise an edge of nervousness in her voice. She felt jumpy and excited, yet fearful that their plan might fail. They'd put so much effort and time into this project. It just had to work.

"All we can do is our best." Tanner used his napkin to wipe a splotch of ketchup off her chin.

She handed him his soda and watched as he took a long drink from the straw. "But what if it fails after all our hard work?"

He took another bite of his burger, chewed and swallowed before responding. "Have a little faith. This is gonna work."

Tanner was telling her to have faith? She was surprised by this turnaround. Maybe she should listen to him. They'd done their best on this project. And with a prayerful heart, she decided to leave the rest up to the Lord.

By six o'clock that evening, bystanders gathered along the river. Farmers and ranchers parked their trucks along the side of the road.

Tanner pointed at the shallow stream. "It looks like the water is starting to rise."

Zoë's heart gave a sudden lurch. "Yes, I think you're right."

Wearing a new set of rubber waders, she walked out into the streambed, pacing impatiently through the murky water. Watching for any signs that the stream might be growing.

And grow it did. Slowly and steadily at first, meandering as it soaked into the partially cracked dirt. Then it gained momentum, the water rushing fast. By nine in the evening, the lower seven miles of the river went from just a trickle to running water at thigh level. But they hadn't reached success yet. Not until the salmon appeared.

They radioed to the Fish and Game to open the fish trap. About an hour later, they turned on the floodlights and waited. The white plastic background would make it easy to see any fish passing by.

Tanner joined Zoë in the river, wearing a pair of hip waders to cover his green Forest Service pants. "Any sign of fish yet?"

Shaking her head, she shielded her eyes from the bright beams of light. She gazed at the shadowed stream. Watching. Waiting. Holding her breath.

Debbie and Blaine Milan waved from the shore to get Zoë's attention. They'd brought their children and Jonah to see this amazing event.

"Mom!" Jonah called.

Zoë waded over to her son, but Tanner beat her there.

"Hi, Jonah. You want to see the fish with us?"

"Sure!"

"I want to come, too," Billie said.

Tanner looked at Blaine. "Is it okay?"

Blaine nodded his permission.

Without another word, Tanner picked up the two boys, one in each arm, and sloshed through the water as he carried them to the middle of the stream. The boys wrapped their arms tightly around his neck and grinned from ear to ear.

"I hope they're not disappointed," Zoë told Debbie. "Our plan may not work."

Debbie shifted the baby in her arms. "It'll work. Tanner sure seems to like kids," Debbie observed, her gaze pinned on the tall man.

He braced his legs apart against the current rushing against his knees and laughed. Seeming very much at home with the little boys.

Zoë nodded. A feeling of warmth flooded her chest as she watched Tanner interact with her son. "Our boys are easy to love."

Debbie's gaze settled on Zoë. "He seems to care a lot for you, too."

Zoë didn't pretend not to understand. "Stop your matchmaking. We're just friends."

Debbie made a face. "Yeah, right."

Zoë ignored this. She remembered what being in love with someone who loved her back felt like and couldn't help wishing she could experience that again. Whatever the outcome of their river project, she loved sharing this experience with Tanner and her little boy. It'd be so easy to become a real family, if only they lived in the same town permanently.

Cameras flashed, the noise of the crowd growing louder. A news crew set up their broadcast nearby, interviewing Chuck Daniels, the forest supervisor. Tanner sloshed back to the shore, setting the kids down.

"Sorry, boys, but my arms are ready to give out," he admitted with a laugh.

"Thanks, Tanner. It was great," Billie said.

Jonah grinned at Billie. "Yeah, none of the other kids got to go out in the river."

Billie reached up and took the baby from his mother's arms. Jonah followed as they sat down on a blanket Debbie had laid out for them and chatted animatedly as they watched the proceedings.

"Thanks for watching Jonah for me," Zoë said to Debbie.

"You're welcome. I know you'll pay me back Friday night when Blaine takes me to the movies."

Debbie went to sit with the children, giving Zoë some time alone with Tanner.

Tanner glanced at Chuck and the news

crew. "They should be interviewing you. This was your idea, but Chuck will undoubtedly get all the recognition."

Zoë shrugged, knowing that was how these things worked. They were the worker bees who came up with the idea and put the plan into action, but the big boss usually got all the credit. "I don't mind, as long as I get to include it on my résumé and share the experience with you."

Tanner met her gaze. "I feel the same. By the way, I've planned our kayaking trip for next week."

"Good. I'll be ready."

Whisper Creek was the final tributary he planned to show her before their summer work project ended in three short weeks. The thought of not seeing him again once their work was finished brought Zoë an overwhelming sense of loss.

She followed as he trudged back into the river. The water level had risen to her midthighs, the current moving much more swiftly now. They stood there gazing at the water, watching for any signs of fish.

"There!" Tanner pointed as the undulating body of a steelhead darted past.

"I saw it. A giant. At least sixteen inches long," Zoë exclaimed with a laugh.

"Maybe more."

The fish headed upstream toward the various tributaries branching off from the river. If there was one fish, perhaps there would be more to come.

Shifting her weight, Zoë's foot sank into the mud of the river bottom and she stumbled. Tanner shot out an arm to catch her. In the eerie shadows, she gazed up into his eyes. Their noses almost touched. Time stood still. The rush of the river filled her ears.

"You okay?"

"Yes." She barely heard his low voice above the rush of water. He released her arms and stepped back, turning his head down to watch for fish.

He pointed again and again. "There!"

"How wonderful." Zoë's voice sounded shrill with delight.

Hearing their excitement, the video operator turned the lens on the spot where they'd seen the fish. Too late. The steelhead was gone. But more soon came in its place. Salmon and trout. Tanner's deep laugh mingled with hers as the fish swarmed past, bumping against their legs.

Without thinking, she linked her arm with his and hugged him tight. Tanner gave a low grunt and she let him go. He might think she was being forward, but she didn't care. It'd been a long time since she'd felt happy, and she wanted to share this moment of triumph with him.

"I'm so proud of you," he whispered against her ear.

Her stomach fluttered. "Thank you. I can't tell you how much that means to me."

"Hey, Tanner. Come on in."

They turned and saw Chuck waving to them from the shore.

Tanner heaved a sigh of satisfaction and gazed at the water swirling around his knees. "Looks like I've been summoned.

I guess it's time to go to shore, unless we want to start swimming."

"I guess so."

He reached for her hand, gripping her fingers tight. As they plowed through the water and up the muddy shore, he steadied her. Rivulets of water drained off their waders as they climbed to dry ground.

Without another word, he headed toward Chuck. Zoë joined the Milans, enjoying their animated conversation as they asked her about the river project. She'd come to Steelhead to make a difference for the endangered fish and she'd done her job. Her success gave her a deep satisfaction for what she and Tanner had accomplished here tonight.

The summer was almost over. Their kayaking trip would be their last excursion together. She and Jonah would move on, but she didn't want to leave.

As she loaded Jonah into the Milans' car and kissed him goodbye, she knew she'd see him again in a few more hours. But Tanner was different. Once she left

Steelhead, she wouldn't see him again. In retrospect, she was glad she hadn't gotten closer to him. A romantic involvement would only complicate her life. Yet, when she contemplated boxing up her home and returning to Portland, she felt as if she was losing something very important to her. And she knew what that something was.

Her best friend.

Where was she? Tanner craned his neck, looking through the crowd, searching for Zoë.

"Let me find her," he told the news reporter. "This was all her idea and I'd like her to speak with you about it."

The reporter waved his hand, looking uninterested. "Never mind. I've got everything I need for my report. I'm heading back to the newsroom now to get this story in for the ten-o'clock news. I can't wait any longer."

"But Zoë Lawton is the one you should be interviewing. This whole project was her idea from the start. She did most of the planning and the work."

The reporter ignored him, turning toward the news van while the cameraman gathered up his equipment.

Tanner whirled around, his gaze scanning the crowds of people on the shore. Desperate to find Zoë. He wanted to share this moment with her. He wanted to share everything with her. His life, his love.

By the time he found her, the news crew had left. He admired Zoë's delicate silhouette outlined by the dark night sky. Moonlight glimmered off the waves like a zillion tiny diamonds.

"How'd your interview go with the media?" she asked.

In the shadowed darkness, he thought he heard an edge of irritation in her voice, but her face remained calm. "Fine. I tried to find you to participate, but when I turned around, you were gone. The news reporter didn't want to hang around."

Her shoulders tensed and she released

a thin sigh. "Yeah, that's the way it goes sometimes."

He was getting bad vibes here. Gone was the camaraderie they'd shared, and he sensed that something was wrong. Normally he wouldn't care, but this woman's opinions mattered greatly to him. He didn't want to upset her in any way. "Zoë, are you okay?"

"Yeah, I'm dandy." She looked away. "I think I'll check on the camera crew one last time to see how the quality of their footage is turning out. It's almost time to wrap things up."

She walked away before he could reply. He stood there alone, the night wind rustling leaves in the cottonwoods overhead. As he watched her go, he felt lost and lonely. As if he was the only man on earth.

In that moment, he realized that Zoë and Jonah had changed his life. As much as he'd tried, he couldn't go back to the way things had been. He was a better man when he was around them—he couldn't deny it. And yet, they made him remember how fragile life was and how easy it was to crush his heart.

His dilemma had increased. He loved her and wanted to spend the rest of eternity with her. He could live his life alone and empty, or he could ask Zoë to stay. It was that simple. Summer was almost over. He needed to speak his mind soon, before he lost her for good.

Chapter Fourteen

Today was the day. Tanner had it all planned. He'd take Zoë kayaking down Whisper Creek. They'd have a lot of fun on this working trip. He'd packed a simple but delicious lunch for them. And when he brought her home that evening, he'd invite her out to dinner at Fresco's, the only Italian restaurant in town. Over lasagna and drippy candles, he'd tell her how he felt about her and ask her to stay.

Standing in Zoë's living room, he picked up her backpack with one finger, startled by its light weight. "This is all you're taking along?"

She stood before him in bare feet, her

short blond hair spiked at the nape of her neck with a bit of gel. He caught the faint scent of her sweet perfume. She'd brushed her long eyelashes with mascara, her cheeks dusted with a hint of blush. He suspected her styled hair and makeup would be ruined the moment a wave hit her in the face, but he appreciated her efforts just the same. And he couldn't contain a rush of anticipation. He got to spend the entire day with her. Just the two of them.

"And this, too." She handed him a plastic container.

He popped the lid, his mouth salivating as the aroma of cinnamon and sugar wafted through the air. He stared at four huge cinnamon rolls slathered with cream-cheese icing. "Did you make these?"

She nodded, a relaxed smile creasing her lovely mouth as she sat on a kitchen chair. Dressed in a simple green T-shirt and knee-length shorts, she pulled on a pair of lightweight water socks before standing again.

"I'm ready." She gathered up her sunglasses and a Chukar baseball cap from the table.

"Have you got some dry clothes?" he asked, trying not to eye her shapely calves.

"Yep. And an extra pair of shoes, in case one of these gets sucked off by the water."

He understood perfectly. The possibility of rolling in a kayak during their trip meant she might have to swim. Wearing heavy shoes that became waterlogged wasn't fun, but even the lighter water socks and wet-suit booties could still be sucked off a person's foot. "How about some extra towels?"

She nodded and waved a yellow dry bag at him. The watertight bag would keep her towels and extra clothing dry even if her kayak rolled.

"You're sure a light packer." He couldn't help remembering the huge, heavy suitcases Cheryl had insisted on packing when she'd taken him to Oregon to meet her parents.

Zoë shrugged. "I have what I need, even in case of an emergency."

She reached for her house keys and they stepped outside. The screen door clapped closed behind them. After locking up the house, she walked with him down the paved sidewalk to his truck.

"I suppose in our line of work, we learn to pack light," she said. "Besides, I can't carry a ton of stuff with me in the boat. If I roll, it'll all fall out and I'll have to chase it down."

He agreed. And yet, he couldn't help feeling that every time he was with this woman, she found another way to surprise him. He couldn't wait for tonight. He couldn't wait to spend the rest of his life with her.

"Jonah's very upset that he can't come along with us," she said.

At the truck, Tanner took the dry bag from her hands and tossed it in the backseat with his own. "Is he staying with the Milans today?"

She chuckled. "Yes, so that made him

feel a bit better. Blaine's taking them to a kids' movie this afternoon. I'm sure Jonah will stuff himself with popcorn and candy to help himself feel better about missing out on our kayaking trip."

He grunted. "Good. There'll be plenty of time to go kayaking with him later on, when he's older."

As Tanner opened the passenger door for her, he thought about the future and becoming a real family. He wanted their day to be perfect before he popped the question.

She tied the sleeves of her drytop water shirt around her waist. Then she climbed up into the truck, a bit more quiet than usual. What was on her mind?

"I'm glad we decided to take this trip," he confessed, suppressing the urge to blurt out his feelings right now.

"You are, huh?"

He stepped nearer. "Yes, very much."

"Me, too. I like being with you." She rested one hand against his chest, her touch sending shock waves through him.

She met his gaze without flinching. Almost as if she dared him to kiss her. And he wanted to. A mass of whirling tops swarmed within his stomach. He leaned closer, until barely a hairbreadth of space separated their faces.

Tell her now. Tell her you love her.

The words filled his mind, but he resisted. He wanted her to remember this day for the rest of her life. To create a special memory for both of them this evening. "I like being with you, too."

"Well, at least you've finally admitted it. I had my doubts after our first meeting with Harry Ragsdale."

A laugh burst from his throat. "Me, too, but I think you've proven your worth many times over since then. Especially considering the success of our water-irrigation project."

She swatted playfully at his shoulder. "Is that right?"

"Yeah." He ran his thumb over the top of her right hand where the caustic water had burned her. "It looks like you won't have any scarring.

"No. It was superficial. No scars, except for right here." She pointed at a thin white line near her right wrist.

Without thinking, he lifted her hand and placed a gentle kiss there. She responded by squeezing his fingers. As he gazed into her eyes, he felt mesmerized. And before he could think to stop himself, he leaned forward and softly kissed her lips.

She drew back and made a pretense of shifting her weight on the seat. Her pale face heated up like road flares. Shy and nervous. To cover the awkward moment, he pretended to inspect their kayaks one last time.

"Did you ever get the report back on your water samples from Hansen Creek?" he asked.

"Yes, and it's no wonder I got chemical burns from that caustic water. The report showed it was basically the pH balance of battery acid."

"Battery acid!" Tanner cringed before

closing her door and walking around the truck. He climbed into the driver's seat and shook his head, as though he couldn't believe what she'd told him. "At least we now have the ammunition to force the mining company to pay for cleanup."

Zoë snorted. "We both know it'll cost millions to clean up those contaminated tailings. Pollution like that will endure for a thousand years."

"Or more." Glancing in his rearview mirror, he inserted the key and started the ignition. "Let's not let that subject spoil our day."

"You're right. Tell you what. Other than showing me Whisper Creek, let's not discuss work at all. Deal?" She held out her hand.

"Deal." He clasped her fingers, her warm skin soft and fragile against the calloused roughness of his palm. As he headed out of town, his heart beat madly in his chest, a myriad of emotions tugging at his mind. Today, he'd tell her he loved her.

"Do both of these kayaks belong to you?" She jerked her head toward the back of the truck where he'd securely tied the boats.

"Just the blue one. I rented the red one for you. It's a bit shorter than mine, to better match your height." He'd chosen her kayak carefully, a design that would handle narrow rivers and drops.

"Thanks."

They chatted and ate the cinnamon rolls, the thick frosting sweet against his tongue. The highway ran parallel to Bingham River, but Tanner soon exited and took a turn. The asphalt ended abruptly and he slowed down as they traveled along the dirt road leading up to Whisper Creek high in the Bingham Mountains.

"Where will we put into the stream?" she asked, gazing out the window as the beautiful landscape of rushing river and willows flashed past.

"At the headwaters of Rock Creek. From there, we'll float down to Whisper Creek and then to the confluence at Bingham

River. The entire course is only about five miles long."

"What class is it again?"

He understood her question. A class three allowed for some easier routes for kayakers to follow in the water, but a class four got tougher. If a person flipped over and had to swim, it wasn't fun and there was a greater chance of getting hurt.

"It's a two, except midway where we'll pass some steep drops and it becomes a three. But don't worry. The white water doesn't last long and I'll be there to help you through it."

She laughed, the sound high and sweet. "Don't worry about me, buddy. I'm a bit out of practice, but I've run class-five rivers before and held my own. I think I can keep up."

He flashed a grin, enjoying her competitive spirit. She wasn't afraid to try new things and she wasn't a wimpy girl. The fact that she enjoyed the outdoors made her even more appealing. "I expected nothing less from you."

Almost two hours later, Ron Parker, one of Tanner's fishery biologists, met them at the guard station used occasionally by fire, trail and road crews. Since Ron was working on the mountain anyway, he'd agreed to drive them up to their entry point into Rock Creek. Then they'd kayak down to the confluence at Whisper Creek. At their exit spot, they'd be right at Tanner's truck rather than having to hike miles back up with their heavy kayaks in tow.

"Thanks for the ride," Zoë said when Ron dropped them off.

The man grinned, his ears reddening. "You're welcome. Just don't get lost out here in the wilds all alone."

"We won't change our route. If we don't make it home on time, you know where we'll be," Tanner said.

"Yep, I do." Once they assured him they had everything they needed, Ron left them with a wave of his hand.

Getting lost was the last fear on Tanner's mind. He knew these mountains like he knew Zoë's delicate face. But he'd never go off kayaking alone without others knowing where he'd be. It just wasn't safe. Anything could happen. The creeks and rivers were constantly changing. Last year, this had been an easy kayaking course. But heavy rains were known to dislodge big trees and boulders. Above all else, Tanner would keep Zoë safe. Nothing else mattered. Nothing was going to ruin this special day with her.

Zoë couldn't deny a sense of excitement as they unloaded and sorted their gear. It'd been so long since she'd gotten outdoors like this for a bit of fun, and she planned to enjoy it. But Tanner's kiss had caught her off guard. She hadn't expected it and wasn't quite sure what it meant. She'd be a fool not to be aware of the electric attraction between them. It seemed sparks ignited inside her every time she saw him. She loved and admired Tanner, but she saw no way for them to be more than friends.

And that was that.

She did her share of work, hustling to help pack their boats. Tanner showed her a hand-size emergency distress locator beacon called an EPIRB. When activated, a satellite could determine its position and relay that info to a search-and-rescue team.

As an afterthought, she tied a simple rope and throw bag to her own boat before coiling it inside where her feet would go. Down by the water, she quickly took some samples and labeled the glass vials. Then she removed her baseball cap and clipped her helmet beneath her chin. She breathed deeply of the damp, loamy soil. Tall aspens and lodgepole pine sat back from the creek, their leaves rustling overhead as the summer breeze whistled by. "I sure love it here."

"You don't miss Portland?" A tinge of hope threaded through his voice.

She tensed, thinking of the life waiting for her back home. She was going to miss the people here in Steelhead, especially Tanner. The thought of leaving him filled her with a kind of emptiness, but she had no choice. Nothing had come of her job search. "Yes, I miss it, but I love it here, too."

Tanner clipped on his own helmet and secured his life vest. "If you think this is pretty, just wait until you see where we're stopping for lunch. I figured we'd split the trip up and stop to eat about midway."

"Sounds good. I can't wait." And she meant it.

Pulling on her drytop shirt, Zoë fought her way through the tight latex gaskets, which would seal water out and help keep her dry and warm in the cold water. Tanner helped her, his touch soft and warm against her arm. Zipping up her PFD life vest, she watched to make sure he did the same. Though it'd been years since she'd been kayaking with her husband, her old habits came back with ease. Kayaking meant you watched each other's backs. Out here, she and Tanner had only each other to rely on.

While Tanner sat on a rock and exchanged his boots for a pair of water socks, she admired his long legs. Like her, he wore knee-length shorts, his muscular calves dusted with dark hair. As he pulled on his shoes, she doubted he had any idea how attractive she found him.

She looked away, focusing on her own gear. Though she wished things could be different, they would soon travel diverse paths and it'd do no good to torture herself by wanting to be here with him.

"Let's run through our hand signals, just to make sure we're on the same page," Tanner suggested.

Zoë concurred. Once they were in the water, they wouldn't always be able to hear well, but they could see signals. They quickly went through the list of stop, slow down, come ahead and other signs. Then they entered the water.

Tanner went first, sliding down into his kayak. As he quickly paddled out into the shallow creek to wait for Zoë, his boat thumped against the rocks. She slipped into her boat and hooked her legs under the thigh braces. After securing the neoprene spray skirt over the cockpit, she used her pole to push her boat out into the narrow stream.

Looking ahead, she saw Tanner pat the top of his helmet to indicate he was okay and ready to go. She responded in kind and he moved forward.

The crystal clear water poured over stones polished smooth by time. Zoë joined the flow, concentrating on her task. Her boat scraped over rocks and she hit the riverbed with each stroke of her paddle, but the rush of the water pushed her onward. She was glad when the creek widened out and the water depth increased a bit.

For thirty minutes, Zoë worked her arms and hips to keep herself upright, using muscles she'd long forgotten she ever had. Her boat bounced through the frothing water. Though she'd once been an experienced kayaker, she realized she was out of practice. But she was fast remembering.

Even with the swift flow of the current, she couldn't keep up with Tanner. He soon noticed her lagging behind and pulled back, waiting patiently for her. Smiling when she drew near. Never once indicating that she was a burden to him. His consideration caused her heart to give a little jerk. Like Tanner, for so long, she'd relied on no one but herself. It felt good to have him in her life, even if they did have to say goodbye soon.

Down below, the confluence changed and they entered Whisper Creek. Shortly afterward, the water calmed and deepened into a pool the color of root beer. That meant the current below was churning up a lot of sediment. Zoë took a cleansing breath before resting her paddle across her spray skirt. She gazed at the pristine wilderness before taking a quick drink from the water bottle stored in the front of her life vest.

"Are you glad you came?" Tanner asked with a knowing smile.

"Oh, yes. You can't see this view from

the roadway. You have to get out of the car and work to find scenery like this."

He nodded, paddling through the deep water with powerful strokes. His boat surged across the flat surface like a soft caress. For several moments, Zoë admired his strength and skill before returning her attention to her own kayak.

After paddling for a couple of hours, her stomach grumbled and she glanced at her waterproof watch. Almost one o'clock. How had the time whizzed by so fast?

Always conscious of her needs, Tanner lifted his arm and gave her the signal to pull up.

As they exited Whisper Creek, Tanner gave her a broad smile of respect. "You weren't kidding, were you? You really can kayak."

A laugh broke from her throat. "So can you. We'll have to do this again sometime."

She bit her tongue, wishing she hadn't said that. For a short time, she'd forgotten that soon they wouldn't be seeing each other anymore.

He tugged his boat up onto the banks, then came back to help her do the same. "I feared you might not be as good at kayaking as you said and I'd have to pull you out of the water. I didn't want to hike back to my truck on foot."

As she removed her helmet, she frowned. "You mean, you thought I'd lied?"

"No, of course not. But some people exaggerate their skills. I should have known you wouldn't. You don't need coddling. You're very independent. I'm amazed every time I'm with you."

His admission warmed her heart. But sometimes she wished she wasn't so self-reliant. Sometimes she longed for someone else to depend on. "I feel the same about you."

Perhaps she'd divulged too much. She wasn't prepared for what happened next. He released the handle and let her boat fall back to the ground as he stepped near.

Cupping her face with his palm, he leaned in and kissed her softly.

"Thanks for coming up here with me," he whispered against her lips. "I'm having the best time of my life."

She pulled back and took a deep inhale before releasing it. "I've never been anyone's best time before."

He quirked one brow. "What about your husband?"

She hesitated. "Derek was wonderful and I loved him, but...he wasn't you."

He flashed that endearing smile of his. "Thank you. That's the nicest thing anyone's ever said to me."

And that's when the crushing despair filled her heart. He'd kissed her twice now. Without intending it, their relationship had ratcheted up several notches. But she cared too much about him to lead him on. "Tanner, I have to go home to Portland soon. That's where my job is. You know I can't stay, right?"

He gazed into her eyes. "Why not?"

"I don't have a job here. In Portland, I

have a pension plan and health insurance. I have a little boy to think about. I have to go back."

He stepped away and slipped his hands into the pockets of his pants, a sure sign that he was disturbed. He gazed at her, his face devoid of expression. But in his eyes, she saw deep, wrenching pain.

"You can stay," he said. "With your talents, we could find you a good job here in Steelhead. I don't want you to leave."

How she wished it would be that easy to find work. But Steelhead was a small town and not a lot of decent jobs were available. Being with Tanner made her think of new beginnings. Being in love. Being a couple again. But she couldn't abandon her career. She'd worked so hard to get where she was today. She couldn't give that up. Not without another job in the wings. She needed her livelihood. She had to think about Jonah. The only thing that would make this situation worse was if he told her he loved her.

The way she loved him.

"Tanner, I'm sorry, but I can't stay."

Chapter Fifteen

Tanner stepped away from Zoë, his body trembling. He couldn't wrap his mind around her words. He couldn't make sense of it all. If only he'd heard some news about the transfer to Portland he'd applied for. But nothing had come of it. Not one word. Which wasn't a good sign. Without a job, he couldn't support a family. And yet, he couldn't lose Zoë, either. "I'm in love with you. I didn't plan for it to happen, but it did. I don't want you to leave."

There, he'd said it. All of it. Now he waited to see her reaction.

Tears shimmered in her eyes and she shook her head. "Oh, Tanner. I was afraid this would happen. You're so wonderful and easy to love. But we have no future together."

"That's up to us."

"No, I have to go back to Portland. It's my home."

A sick feeling settled in his stomach. "I know we can find you a job here."

She snorted. "I've already tried. There's nothing available in this harsh economy."

"Please, Zoë, won't you give staying a chance—for me? You know I love Jonah. I'll make him a good father. If you'll give us a chance to see where this relationship could go, I'd spend the rest of my life making you happy."

She blinked and released a shuddering breath. "I can't do that, Tanner. I love my job. You have your work here, and mine is in Oregon. Long-distance wouldn't work between us, either."

No, it wouldn't. "Then, I'll come to Portland. I can get another job there."

He hoped.

She stared at him, her eyes widening. "You'd do that for me?"

Leaving the mountain range he loved and living in a large city like Portland didn't appeal to him, but he'd do it to be with the woman he adored. "Yes, I would."

And he meant it. He'd been alone all his life. The job here no longer meant everything to him when faced with the possibility of losing Zoë and Jonah.

She clenched her eyes shut, as if absorbing the impact of his words. "I can't make you do that."

He took a step toward her, wrapping his hands gently around her upper arms. "Why not? Being with you is more important to me than any job."

"It wouldn't be fair. At first, we'd be okay. But what if you weren't happy in another job? After a time, you'd come to resent me for it. Then where would we be?"

He gave a careless laugh. "That wouldn't happen. I'd be with you and Jonah. I can be happy in any job. All you have to say is that you love me, and I'll go anywhere for you."

She opened her mouth as though she wanted to say the words, but then pursed her lips, her face tight with unshed tears. "No, Tanner. I'd feel horrible doing that. It won't work."

"We can make it work, sweetheart. Tell me you love me. That's all I need to hear."

"No." She held up a hand, stopping his advance.

He stood there, longing to take her into his arms and hold her tight.

"So where does that leave us?" he asked.

Her face went pale. "We'll always be good friends."

Friends!

"Is that enough for you?" he asked, unable to hide his incredulity.

"It'll have to be. It's all we can have." Her voice wobbled as she took a deep breath. Then she turned her back on him, busying herself by tying off her boat. "What's the elevation here?"

The elevation? How could she think about elevation when he was dying inside?

Without waiting for his reply, she searched her boat for a waterproof pack with their lunches inside. He stood there staring at her. Aching with loss.

And just like that, she brushed his love aside.

He coughed to clear the lump in his throat, his mind swimming with a barrage of emotion that bludgeoned his heart. This couldn't be it. There had to be more. He didn't know what to think or feel. He felt numb and empty. "The…the elevation at the summit is almost 7,600 feet."

She shivered, her thick voice the only indication that she was still distressed. "Brr. No wonder the water is so cold here. It's filled with snowmelt."

Tanner looked away as she dragged out her sample kit, then dipped her vials into the water and the nutrient-rich mud. She searched the water, looking for fish. He didn't move when she pointed out several. He didn't care anymore. Not when his whole world was caving in.

Trying to calm his nerves, Tanner laid out their picnic, wishing he'd never confided his true feelings to Zoë. He hadn't handled this right. He should have waited until tonight, as he'd planned. But would it have mattered? Her answer would have been the same.

She didn't want him.

The realization battered his brain. He'd taken a leap of faith and been hurt again. And yet, he didn't blame God this time. Nor did he believe the Lord had abandoned him. God was still there, filling Tanner's heart with peace. Zoë's rejection wasn't easy to accept, but he knew everything would be okay. He just didn't understand how.

Once Zoë had finished her work, they sat across from each other, both of them picking at their meat-and-cheese sandwiches.

"I guess I'm not as hungry as I thought," Zoë said.

"Me, either." He dropped his half-eaten brownie onto its plastic wrapper and stood up. He had nothing else to say.

She took a swallow of apple juice, then wrapped her arms around herself and coiled her legs beneath her. Watching her shiver brought out the compassion in him. Whether she wanted him or not, he still loved her. He'd always love her.

Without a word, he removed his jacket and draped it over her shoulders. She nodded her thanks, snuggling deep into the warm folds of fabric. Seeing her wrapped up inside his coat made his heart ache. But more than anything, he wanted her to be happy.

To take his mind off this rotten turn of events, he cleaned up their camp and stowed their gear back inside their boats. As he stepped over to his kayak, Zoë rested her hand on his arm and he paused.

"Tanner, please don't be angry. I didn't mean to hurt you. Can you ever forgive me?"

Searching his heart, he felt no anger. No

bitterness. How could he resent her when he loved her so much? If only it didn't hurt so bad.

He reached out and brushed his fingertips against her warm cheek. "Of course. Don't worry, everything will be fine."

As he stepped past her and slid into his kayak, he hoped he was right. Without another word, he used his paddle to push away and float out into the stream. While he waited for her to join him, the hollow loneliness invaded his mind like an old, comfortable friend.

Zoë regretted how this day had turned out. She'd never forget Tanner's stony look when she'd told him she couldn't stay. But if she'd given their love a chance, how could that ever have worked for them? Two people so set in their careers, with jobs in different states.

It must have been difficult for Tanner to take a second chance on romance. Maybe she shouldn't put her career before love. But she'd learned the hard way that a good job meant food on the table, a roof over her head and security. She couldn't give all that up, for Jonah's sake and her own. Neither could she ask Tanner to abandon his work and follow her to Portland. It wouldn't be fair. He loved her now, but over time, that could change. At least here in Steelhead, he had his job. He'd be busy and forget about her soon enough. She couldn't ask any more.

Because she loved him.

Back on the water, she welcomed the chilly breeze that cooled her flushed face. The river deepened, the push of the current much stronger now. As Zoë dipped her paddle into the water, it no longer hit bottom. The roar of the water swelled and filled her ears. The transparent riffle gave way to churning white water.

Zoë kept up, watching as Tanner pointed to the left or right to indicate a less hazardous path she should take. She never hesitated to follow his direction, trusting him completely.

If she trusted Tanner the way she trusted

the Lord, why couldn't she have more faith in their love? Surely she and Tanner could figure out a way to be together. She racked her brain but found no answers. In order to be together, one of them would have to move. Which would require a giant leap of faith. And that forced Zoë to look deep inside her soul and ask herself if she loved Tanner enough to give up the career she loved. For all her talk about trusting the Lord, her faith had lapsed. Tanner seemed like the strong one now. But she didn't know if his confidence was enough for her.

Instead, she focused on her paddling. She couldn't think about this now. She needed time alone to contemplate what was really important to her. Above all, she wanted no regrets.

Tanner lifted his arm, giving her the signal to pull up and wait. Jagged rocks jutted outward like porcupine spines. An enormous granite boulder blocked their way, creating a swirling vortex in their path. She immediately thrust her paddle into the water and surged forward into a small eddy beside a sharp outcropping of rock.

Tanner circled the whirlpool, casting glances over his shoulder, as if to assure himself that she was okay. And in the process of looking out for her, he jeopardized his own safety.

Zoë watched helplessly as he thrust his paddle to the left, struggling to evade the boulder. He tried to straighten on the right, but his boat jerked back. Water pummeled his spray skirt, forcing his head down so his helmet banged against the boat. His kayak spun around, his face beneath the foaming water. The sickening sound of his helmet striking the rock again filled her ears. And then she saw his helmet floating away, bouncing along on the current as though it hadn't a care in the world. A rivet on his chin strap must have broken. His paddle followed suit, racing beyond reach.

She bit back a scream. "Tanner!"

He hung limp within his boat as it spun

around, suspended within the whirlpool. A swell of white water rushed over his prow, striking him in the face.

"Tanner! Can you swim?" she yelled, hoping he could hear her.

She patted her helmet over and over again, to see if he'd respond and indicate he was okay, but she knew it was futile. He didn't need to show any hand signals to tell her he was in trouble.

Please, God! Help us.

She whispered the prayer in her heart as Tanner sat up groggily, weaving back and forth like a rag doll. She couldn't understand why his kayak didn't roll and drown him. The powers of physics defied any reasoning. By all accounts, he should be upside down in the water.

A stream of crimson poured over his forehead and down his right temple. He was wounded! Thank Heaven his boat wasn't going anywhere. It seemed stuck tight against the churning blur of the whirlpool.

Using her paddle like a spear, Zoë thrust

it deep into the river bottom to serve as an anchor. It'd do no good to speak and try to tell Tanner what she planned. Neither of them could hear above the crashing waves. But he was watching her, his amber eyes hooded and blinking, as though he was fighting to stay awake. Yet he couldn't move. Couldn't do anything to help himself.

Undoubtedly, he had a head injury. Just how bad, she wasn't sure. She had to get him to safety before he passed out and drowned.

She reached forward and popped off the spray skirt of her boat, then jerked up the length of rope she'd had the foresight to include at the beginning of their trip. She tossed him the line, amazed when he caught the throw bag and had the presence of mind to twist the rope around his wrist for a firm hold.

Zoë hooked one of her arms around her paddle to hold herself in place. With a gargantuan effort, she pulled on the line—not an easy feat with one hand. Tanner held on tight to the rope. Hand over hand, she fought to reel him in. Her arms burned like liquid fire. As his kayak inched toward the eddy, her entire body shook from her exertions. She breathed in hard, her lungs aching.

His kayak finally slid into the eddy next to her. The two fiberglass boats thumped against each other, her kayak jerking back. The heavy current drummed against her prow, but she held there, poised along the eddy line.

"Are you okay?" She reached for him, holding on to his arm.

He slumped over, his strength finally spent. He almost capsized his boat. She grabbed and pulled hard to keep him upright. If he rolled in this condition, he'd drown. She wouldn't be able to save him.

"Come on! Stay with me," she demanded, yelling loudly.

"Zoë, you okay…?" He blinked, his eyes glassy and dazed. His arms hung limp. He was barely holding on.

"Yes, I'm fine. It's you I'm worried about."

He didn't seem to hear. He kept repeating the same question over and over again. His eyes were open, but he wasn't acting right. As though his fear for her was the only thing keeping him conscious.

It took a good fifteen minutes of precious time for her to keep him upright while moving her kayak into a position so she could safely exit her boat.

She tugged on Tanner, pulling him free of his kayak. He wasn't totally deadweight, but almost. If he'd been completely unconscious, she wouldn't have been able to get him to shore. At her urging, he leveraged his legs, helping lift himself out of the boat.

She let him rest where he fell on the shore, moving sticks and rocks away from digging into his back. Within minutes, she had him wrapped in every single towel and piece of warm clothing she could find inside their boats. Gazing at the dusky sky, she figured they were no more than two miles away from his truck. It might just as well have been a thousand miles. Though it'd be a long, difficult hike through raw wilderness, she could do it, but Tanner couldn't. Fearing he might die, she wouldn't leave him alone. She didn't dare. Hopefully, a rescue team would find them before long.

Instead, she offered first aid the only way she knew how. Applying light pressure to the deep gash along the edge of his hairline, she elevated his head slightly and kept him quiet and still. Then she turned on the EPIRB tracking system.

She was supposed to pick up Jonah from the Milans' by six o'clock that evening. Zoë figured Debbie would wait another two hours after that to make sure Zoë wasn't just running late before she called Ron Parker. Ron knew where they were and would call out a rescue team. If Ron followed the creek, it'd be easy enough to find them. But Zoë and Tanner would have to wait until someone missed them first. And that could take quite a few hours.

Tanner might die!

A blaze of terror tore through her and she rubbed her hands over his arms to warm him. Memories of holding Derek after his skiing accident flooded her mind. The blood streaming from his head. His ashen face and hooded eyes. And then his lifeless body as she waited for someone to come help them.

Dear Lord, help us. I can't go through this again!

She shook with reaction, struggling not to give in to her fear. Trying to hold herself together. Tanner needed her now. She mustn't panic.

"Don't go to sleep. Please, don't go to sleep," she begged him when he closed his eyes for the umpteenth time.

"Sorry…this…happened…"

"There's no need to apologize. Just stay awake."

"So…tired…"

"I know, but you've got to stay awake.

You'll scare me to death if you fall asleep now."

"Don't…mean…to…scare…you…" His speech sounded awkward and slurred.

Just like Derek.

She kept Tanner talking. Kept him thinking, even as she kept him calm. She asked about his childhood and college life, even making him tell her details about his grandparents. Once the wound on his head stopped bleeding, she elevated his feet to prevent him from going into shock.

For three hours, she stayed with him, brushing her fingers against the stubble on his cheek, over and over again, to assure him she wouldn't leave him. Ensuring he was peaceful and warm. Reassuring herself that he hadn't died.

By nightfall, even the summer sunlight couldn't keep them from freezing in these mountains, and she was forced to build a fire. Relying on the survival skills she'd learned over the years, she quickly gathered stones to create a ring and then piled up dried sticks and kindling. The disposable lighter she kept in her supplies for just such an emergency made quick work of the chore and she soon had a cheery campfire to keep them warm.

"Thank you," Tanner murmured, his shadowed gaze following her with a bit more lucidity.

She shuddered with relief. He hadn't died and seemed to be more alert now. "You're welcome."

She loved him. She couldn't deny it. Her feelings swamped her with emotion so powerful she had to blink. Her love for this man had been growing all summer long. She'd spent so much time working with him, but she'd tried to take it slow. With a child to think about, she wanted something permanent and lasting in her life. She'd settle for nothing less.

She loved him and might lose him.

"You just stay with me, okay?" She tried to smile, to reassure him.

"Forever," he vowed.

The word sank deep into her heart. She needed this man. Needed his love. But right now, she could only think about saving his life.

He returned her smile and she thought he was doing better. Speaking more clearly. Moving his hands and legs more frequently. But she still didn't let down her guard. If he were hemorrhaging inside, Tanner could still die. And so she used the only weapon she had to fight her fears and doubts. She exercised her faith and prayed.

Chapter Sixteen

Tanner blinked his eyes open. A spear of pain pierced his head. He focused on the window where sunlight streamed past the white plastic blinds. His arms and legs felt heavy. Lethargic. As if they weighed a million tons. He fought off the groggy exhaustion, trying to remember where he was. Trying to remember what had happened—

"Zoë!" On the river. The whirlpool. Danger.

He tried to sit up, but something pressed him back.

"Shh, just lie still, now."

He gazed up at a nurse with cheery

cheeks and a calming smile. She pressed her hand against his shoulder and he lay back in the hospital bed. The name badge pinned to her white smock read Sharon.

"Where...?" he swallowed against his dry throat and tried again. "Where am I?"

A *bleep* sounded and he stared at a variety of blinking monitors nearby. An IV tube had tangled around his hand. He pulled against the weight, a blaze of panic rushing through him.

"Hold still, now. I'll take care of that for you." Sharon steadied his arm and quickly disentangled the contraption. While she smoothed her fingers across the tape holding the needle in his arm, he fought off the urge to bolt from the bed.

"Where am I?" he asked again.

"Steelhead Memorial Hospital. You got quite a bump on the head." She adjusted the IV drip before leaning close and flashing a beam of light into his eyes.

He blinked.

"Where's Zoë?" His voice sounded like rough sandpaper rasping against wood.

Sharon stood back and jotted some notes on a clipboard. "You mean the woman who was with you on the river?"

He nodded, the movement making his head spin. A bout of nausea forced him to shut his eyes for several moments. He lifted his free hand, his fingertips pressing against a bandage wrapped around his forehead.

"She went home to get some rest," Sharon said.

"She…she's okay, then?"

The nurse adjusted his pillows. "She was just fine last time I saw her an hour ago. She wouldn't leave your side all night, until she knew you were gonna be okay. I finally convinced her to go home and get some sleep."

Zoë had been here with him. She was okay.

He relaxed, coughing to clear his rusty voice. "What happened to me?"

"You conked your head on a big rock. Do you recall any of it?"

He closed his eyes, the roar of the river filling his memory along with grinding fear that Zoë might get caught in the whirlpool, her kayak would flip over and she'd drown. He'd been filled with clenching terror. And he'd prayed, for the first time in two years. Asking God to help them. To keep them safe. In the process of watching out for Zoë, he'd grown careless with his own boat and had ended up being knocked out cold. "Yes, I remember. We were kayaking."

"That's right. And lucky for you, your friend pulled you from the water and stayed with you until the rescue team arrived. From what I've heard, it was a long night for everyone, but she saved your life."

He vaguely remembered the freezing cold. The confusion. The helplessness. And Zoë leaning over him, her blue eyes creased with worry as she tucked towels and jackets around him. Her gentle touch as she'd caressed his face, insisting he stay awake and talk to her. What he'd said to her, he had no idea. But he remembered the warmth of her soft hands against his icy cheeks and the soothing reassurance of her voice.

She'd saved his life. He owed everything to her. If only she could love him the way that he loved her.

"I'll let the doctor know you're awake." Sharon headed for the door, leaving him alone for several minutes.

So much for him being the big, strong male. Zoë had pulled him from the river and kept him alive. If not for her quick thinking, he would have died. He could barely wait to speak with her. To find out what had happened and how long it'd taken the rescue team to find them.

He could hardly believe what Zoë had done. Hardly grasp her inner willpower and determination to succeed. Strong, yet gentle. Resolute and courageous.

This wasn't the first time she'd had to be strong. After her husband died, she'd made her own way in the world. She'd built a life for herself and a stable home for Jonah. She didn't need Tanner or any man. He couldn't blame her for not wanting to give that life up on the chance that they could make their fledgling relationship last.

Life was hard and full of uncertainties. There were no guarantees they'd never be disappointed or hurt. No guarantees they'd always be happy.

Tanner knew only one thing. He loved her and it didn't matter. He'd lost her anyway.

She shouldn't have come here. Zoë stood before the door of Tanner's hospital room, her pulse hammering against her temples. After what had happened on the river, she couldn't stop thinking about how she'd almost lost him. In spite of her inner resolve, she'd been shaken up pretty badly.

Her love for Tanner had brought her

here. She had to know that he was really okay. That he'd make a full recovery.

She rapped her knuckles against the door, then peeked inside. Tanner was sitting up in bed. He turned to look at her, a smile widening across his face when he saw her.

"Zoë!"

She returned his smile, walking to his side, feeling cautious and withdrawn. "Hi, Tanner. You're looking more chipper than the last time I saw you earlier this morning. You doing okay?"

She longed to give him a hug, but fought off the urge.

"I can't tell you how grateful I am for what you did for me." His voice sounded thick with emotion.

She jerked one shoulder. "I did what anyone would do."

"No, not just anyone. You saved my life. Thank you, Zoë."

A flood of emotion almost overwhelmed her. Flashes of his pale face and glazed eyes filled her mind. By the grace of God, he'd survived.

"You're welcome." She dragged her hand away and took one step back. Wishing things could be different between them. Wishing they weren't two lost souls.

He frowned, his amber eyes boring into hers like a high-speed drill. "What's wrong?"

"Nothing." *Everything!*

"Are you sure you're okay?" he asked.

"Yeah, I am now that I know you're going to be all right. You had me scared there for a time."

He gave a low chuckle. "Truthfully, I kind of scared myself. I'm sorry about that. We were having a lot of fun...until I tried to break a rock with my head."

She didn't laugh. A frenzy of heat flooded her face. She forced a stiff smile to her lips but couldn't stop thinking about their discussion before the accident.

"What happened after I conked my head?" he asked.

She told him about their rescue. As she'd

predicted, Debbie had called Ron to report that Zoë had never picked up Jonah. Ron had immediately called out a rescue team, which had located Tanner and Zoë just after midnight. They'd rushed Tanner to the hospital where Zoë had paced the floor, praying he wouldn't die.

"I'm sorry you had to go through all that," he said.

"You would have done the same for me."

"Yes, I would. I'm just glad you weren't hurt."

"No, I'm fine." What more could she say? Nothing had changed between them. They'd become close, and yet the barriers had become even higher and more solid.

"How's Jonah?" he asked.

"Good. He keeps asking about you." Maybe she shouldn't have said that. Above all else, she must protect her son from being hurt. Hanging out with Tanner had been good for the boy, but now it was time to pull back.

"I'd like to see him, too. Maybe we can go fishing again."

"Maybe." Pain and regret stabbed holes in her heart. Sometimes love was not enough.

He must have sensed her reservations because he frowned. "You sure you're all right, Zoë?"

No, she wasn't sure at all.

She took a deep, settling breath. "I've learned so much from you, Tanner. You taught me when to be tough and when to let it go and work things out. Thank you for that."

Tenderness filled his eyes. "You've taught me the same things. I meant what I said on the river. I haven't changed my mind about us."

Her heart gave a sharp flutter. She almost told him that she'd change *her* mind, that she wanted to take that leap of faith, but couldn't seem to do so. She'd always thought she was so strong, but now she realized she wasn't. Not at all. "Right now, I just want you to get some rest."

He nodded, his gaze caressing her face, but he didn't say any more. His jaw hardened. A horrible, swelling silence followed. She waited for him to say something, anything, that would give her an indication that he could forgive her.

She decided to change the subject. "Well, I'd better get going. I'm heading into the office to start writing my final report on our work this summer."

"Good. They're talking about letting me go home tomorrow, so I'll be able to help compile the research then."

"I'll...I'll let your assistant know what I'm planning. It shouldn't take long to get a first draft finished."

"I'll call you tomorrow," he said.

She gave him a half smile before leaning close and kissing him on the cheek. As she drew back, she avoided his eyes. "You take care of yourself, okay?"

"Yeah, you, too."

And that was it. She turned and left the room. Standing against the wall in the stairwell, she tried to still her racing pulse. She hadn't told Tanner she loved him. She didn't dare. Because that would make leaving him even more difficult.

Tanner lay there stunned and confused after Zoë left. He felt empty inside. What had happened? Things hadn't gone as he'd envisioned them. He'd confessed his love, but it hadn't been enough.

Tanner would willingly give up his job here in Steelhead, but Zoë was right. The job market was tight right now. If he failed to find a decent-paying job, he'd feel like a failure. If he and Zoë eventually married, he'd want to provide for his family. To take care of them. Maybe he was old-fashioned, but that was how it must be for him. So where did that leave them?

He could see no way out of this dilemma. No way for them to be together.

And then a thought struck him. If God could bring such a wonderful woman to him, then surely the Lord would help them find a way to be together. It was a righteous desire, after all. Tanner thought he just needed to have faith. But how should he begin?

Something told him he should start with prayer. Hmm. Now, that was something to think about.

Chapter Seventeen

Zoë dropped the heavy box. It hit the cement floor of her garage with a thud. Blowing a short strand of hair out of her eyes, she scooted the box over to the far wall with her foot. A fall breeze rushed past, blowing yellow-and-red leaves inside along with a swirl of dust. She'd have to sweep it all out later.

She shivered and zipped up her light jacket. After the busy summer she'd had, it was time to pack again. Not a chore she relished in the least. She eyed the dirt, leaves and oil splotches marring the cement floor. On her way over to pick up Jonah from the Milans' house, she'd stop at the hardware store and buy a canister of grease cleaner.

Then she wondered why she bothered. Tanner was gone from her life, seeming to take all her joy with him. Returning to Oregon provided her with the employment she loved and needed, yet little else. No more joy. No love. Even Jonah was in a funk, knowing he'd have to leave Billie.

She didn't want to go, but she had no choice. Her efforts to find a job here in Steelhead had proven fruitless.

And maybe it was for the best. Everywhere she looked, places reminded her of Tanner. The mountains, the river, Kids' Creek Park, even the grocery store. How could she forget and move on without him?

Her mind struggled to find a way for them to be together, but she couldn't see any. No matter what they did, one of them would be without a job.

Dressed in worn blue jeans, tennis shoes and an old gray sweatshirt, she swiped an arm across her forehead. Her gaze scanned the piles of cardboard boxes and she decided to label them so she'd know their contents. She'd been so rushed when she first moved to Steelhead. Never enough time. Now her days seemed to drag by. She missed Tanner. His smile, his low voice, his intelligent mind.

Reaching for another flat box sitting on top of the freezer, she folded the flaps and taped them in preparation for packing. Working kept her mind off her broken heart. No matter how hard she'd tried, she couldn't stop loving Tanner. Over the past few weeks, she'd finished her final fishery report, sending it to him via email. He'd made his sterile, professional comments in writing. No phone calls. No personal interaction.

Nothing.

He obviously didn't want to see her again. And she couldn't blame him. She'd picked up the phone several times to call him and had even driven by his office, longing to talk about nothing and everything. But she couldn't. It'd only deepen their pain.

Poor Jonah. No matter how many days passed, he kept asking to see Tanner. He wanted to go fishing again and invite Tanner to his T-ball games. The little boy didn't understand why the man didn't come around anymore. Why he never called. Jonah thought he'd done something wrong. It almost broke Zoë's heart to tell her son it wasn't his fault. It wasn't anyone's fault.

Sometimes life could be so complicated.

As she folded a tattered blanket, she remembered Tanner's tilted smile. The way the sunlight glinted off his dark hair. The way his amber eyes creased with thought. The firm line of his jaw and the way he walked, so confident and self-assured, as though he—

"Zoë?"

She turned and found him standing behind her. At first, she thought he was a mirage. A figment of her imagination.

The garage door stood wide open, letting sunlight and wind flow into the room. In the murky shadows, she blinked several times and shook her head.

"I hope I'm not interrupting anything important." He nodded at the grimy cleaning rag she held in her left hand and she dropped it to the floor.

"Tanner." She barely got the word out around the hard lump in her throat.

"Hi there." He spoke softly, calm as a summer's morning.

All she could think about at that moment was how wonderful his deep voice sounded. As she gazed into his eyes, she felt mesmerized. Frozen in place for fear that he might disappear. Then she noticed he was wearing his best Sunday suit of clothes. No blue jeans and no Forest Service uniform today. Just a white shirt, yellow tie and his shiny wing-tip shoes.

"You look good," she murmured.

"Thanks. So do you. Absolutely beautiful, as always."

She widened her eyes, thinking she must look awful with no makeup and wearing her grungy work clothes. Just like that first day they'd met.

"Wh…what are you doing here?" Her voice sounded vague to her ears, as though she spoke from a tunnel. She couldn't believe he was really here.

"I came to see you. I hope that's okay."

"Yes, of course. Would you like to come inside? I'm afraid Jonah's not here."

She turned and headed toward the doorway leading into the kitchen, walking on autopilot. Afraid she might start bawling like a baby and beg him to ask her to stay just one more time.

Her spine tensed and she clenched her hands, her nerves tight as a bowstring. Why had he come here?

Tanner followed her inside and stood beside the fridge, his tall, lean body seeming to fill up the kitchen, bigger than life itself.

He smiled, seeming so at ease when her body was a mass of jittery nerves. "Let me guess. Jonah's over at the Milans'."

She nodded, captivated by his presence

so close at hand. And then she noticed the flowers he held. Red roses wrapped in green tissue paper. At least two dozen of them.

"These are for you." He held them out.

She took the flowers dumbly, cradling them in her arms, pressing her nose in close to catch their velvety fragrance. "Thank you, but what are they for?"

"Because I love you. More than I can ever say."

She staggered, her body trembling. Sudden tears burned the backs of her eyes. She blinked to keep them from falling. "Tanner, I can't take this anymore. Please, don't—"

He held up a hand, his eyes crinkled in a serious expression. "Before you speak, I have something very important I want to say."

He stepped close. He didn't touch her, but she felt the warmth of his body seeping into hers. He slid one of his hands into the pocket of his suit coat and pulled out two white envelopes.

"I don't understand." Her legs wobbled with reaction. What was he doing here, dressed so handsome and smelling so good? She regretted hurting him, the way Cheryl had hurt him. It was already too late. Zoë had fallen in love with him and had been suffering from a broken heart since she'd turned him down.

"Let me explain, Zoë. You see, since the kayaking accident, I've been doing a lot of thinking and working some things out in my mind. Things that have troubled me for way too long now."

"What things?"

"My relationship with God, my priorities…and you."

Her heart tripped over itself as she gazed into his eyes. She couldn't speak, but held her breath.

"The kayaking accident made me realize how fragile life is, for all of us. I could have lost you forever. And I finally came to several important realizations."

She swallowed hard. "Such as?"

"First, I know God has never abandoned me. No matter how alone I've been throughout my life, He's always been there, waiting for me to return to Him. I've lost a lot in my life, but it's made me stronger. It's made me the person I am today. God loves all of us. He wants us to be happy. You taught me that."

"I...I did?"

He nodded. "So I had some intense discussions with the Lord about everything. The Gospel of Jesus Christ makes me want to be a better man. For you. And Jonah. And when I realized that, nothing else mattered except being with the ones I love. I feel so calm inside. I can finally accept everything and move on."

She released a shaky breath. "Oh, Tanner, I'm so glad. So very glad."

"I know now that God has something better in mind for me. And that something is you."

Zoë looked down, feeling overwhelmed. Why did he have to say such things? It only made the situation more difficult for both of them.

He stepped nearer, placing his finger beneath her chin and gently lifting her face so she looked into his eyes. A tender smile creased his handsome mouth, his voice whisper-soft. "I must have loved you from the first moment I saw you in that parking lot after Jonah creamed my truck with your shopping cart. After I found out you were planning to move back to Portland, I kept pushing my feelings aside. I thought I could pretend I didn't love you. That if I avoided admitting the truth, I'd feel happier inside. I'd protect myself from being hurt again and you'd just leave at the end of the summer. End of story."

She licked her upper lip, her entire body shaking. "And have you felt happier?"

He shook his head, cupping her cheek with the warmth of his palm. "No. In fact, I'm miserable without you. I can't eat or sleep. All I do is think about you. I miss our trips into the mountains. I miss fishing with Jonah. I want to go kayaking with you again, without the accident this time. I love you so much. I can't think of living the rest of my life without you."

She gave a croaking laugh and pulled a kitchen chair out. She plopped down, too weak to stand. Too overcome by emotion to fight him anymore.

"And so I decided to fight for a chance for us," he said. "I've waited all my life for you, and I'm not gonna sit by and watch you walk away from me. No matter what, we belong together. Nothing else matters. Not my job, or where I live, or what I eat for dinner. All that matters is us, lady. We just need to have faith in that, and everything will be all right."

Her heart squeezed and she no longer fought the barrage of tears flowing down her cheeks.

He knelt before her, taking her hands in his. She stared into his eyes, too nervous to speak. Afraid he might evaporate from her sight.

"And so it comes down to this." He held out the two envelopes. "Pick one."

"Wh...what are they?"

He lifted one that had her name scrawled across it in bold writing. "This is a letter to you from your boss in Portland. He couldn't be here, so he called Chuck and he asked me to deliver it to you in his place. Apparently, you applied for a lower-level job here in Steelhead, but they felt you were overqualified, so you didn't get the position. But your boss in Portland is so pleased by your success here with the water-irrigation project that he wants you to stay permanently. You'd have your same job, but it'd be here in Steelhead."

A tremor swept her body as Tanner held up the other envelope. It was addressed to him. "And this one is a copy of a job offer for me in the Portland regional office."

"But...but how did you get a job there?"

He flashed a dazzling smile. "I applied for it weeks ago. I don't care where I work, but I'm determined to be with you. So, now you have a choice to make. Where are we going to live? I'll stay in a pup tent down in the park, if that's what you want.

As long as I can spend time with you and Jonah."

The ramifications of his words settled over her by slow degrees. She took both envelopes, opening and reading each letter, trying to comprehend what was happening. Then she took a shuddering breath. "Let me make sure I understand. You requested a transfer to Portland?"

He nodded, not looking flustered in the least. "Just like you put in for a transfer here to Steelhead."

"And I can have my same job here in Steelhead?" she said.

Another nod.

A slightly hysterical laugh burst from her throat. He laughed, too, at the irony of it all. And then he took her hand in his.

"Apparently, we've both been working behind the scenes to get new jobs. I never saw this turn of events coming, but the Lord provided us with options on ways to be together," he said.

"But now you have a transfer to Portland."

He shrugged. "I can change my mind and stop the transfer, but only if it's what you want. Do you mind staying here in Steelhead, or do you want to live in Portland?"

She didn't even hesitate. "Steelhead, obviously. Jonah's so happy here, and so am I. Oh, Tanner. This is too good to be true. I can't believe it."

She threw her arms around his neck and hugged him tight. And when she drew back, she saw that he was smiling, too.

"When I received your letter from Portland this morning with a request to deliver it to you, I couldn't believe our good fortune. Several weeks ago, I told the Lord our problem and asked Him for help. I decided to exercise faith, and this is what came of it. We both have jobs here in Steelhead. Nothing's holding us back any longer."

The chair creaked as she sat forward. Stunned. Charmed. And shaking like a leaf.

"You're the woman for me, Zoë. I love you. I always have."

"Oh, Tanner. I'm so sorry I ever doubted we could work this out. I've felt awful. I didn't know how I was going to move back to Portland without you. For the first time, I actually began to hate my job."

"And now you won't have to go." He withdrew a black velvet box from his pocket. When he popped the lid open, she blinked, hardly able to believe her eyes. Sitting on the satin bedding was a lovely diamond ring, modest and beautiful in its simplicity.

"It's not the Hope Diamond, but there's a lot of hope in it anyway. For us. For our future. For our family." He paused for several heartbeats. "Marry me, Zoë. Marry me and make me the happiest man in the world."

As he removed the ring and reached for her left hand, she inhaled a shaky breath.

"May I?" he asked, his face filled with anticipation.

Her mind whirled. She couldn't believe this was happening. It was a dream. Wishful thinking. Anytime now, she'd wake up and it wouldn't be real. He wanted permission to put his ring on her finger. Permission to marry her.

"Yes," she barely whispered, and then more strongly, "oh, yes, Tanner."

And then she laughed as he slid the ring onto her fourth finger, a perfect fit. She wrapped her arms around his neck and kissed him. Holding nothing back. No more doubts, no more denials. The walls were broken down. She and Tanner no longer needed to hide or pretend.

Love had found them and healed their broken hearts. The Lord had opened the way.

Tanner pulled her close, murmuring that he adored her. Telling her how much he'd missed her these past few weeks. Asking her forgiveness for ever doubting the Lord.

She drew back just enough for their noses to touch, ignoring the tears of happiness sliding down her cheeks. "I love you, Tanner. I've been so unhappy with you gone. I didn't know what I was going to do. Both Jonah and I have missed you so much."

A deep chuckle shook his chest. "I can't resist that little guy. Nor can I resist you. Not ever again, honey."

Honey. One of the sweetest names she'd ever been called. They kissed again, promising to cleave unto one another forever. Making plans for a quick wedding date.

"No more waiting for me," he said.

"Or me, either. Thank you for saving me," she said.

He tilted his head to one side. "From what?"

"From Paul Carter. Since you've been gone, he calls me two or three times a week, sometimes even showing up on my doorstep to ask me out. Jonah's gotten quite rude with him. He actually slammed the door in Paul's face last night. Then he informed me that if I wasn't going to marry you, he was now the man of the house and Paul isn't allowed inside our home ever again. Can you imagine that?"

Tanner threw back his head and laughed long and hard. "That's my boy."

Zoë snorted. "It's not funny. I've been in real trouble with Paul. He's even planning to move to Portland because he thinks I'll be there."

"Let him." Tanner reached out a hand and cupped her cheek, his touch so tender as he smiled into her eyes. "Paul won't be a problem anymore. Not with my ring on your finger. We'll announce our engagement to the entire congregation at church on Sunday. He'll back off. I guarantee it."

Yes! This was what she wanted. What she needed. Tanner to love her. Tanner to share her life.

His eyes gleamed with joy. "Would you mind if we went and got Jonah now? I need to ask his permission to marry you. Hopefully, he'll approve."

"Yes, he will."

"I think a celebration is in order and I'd like to share this great news with our little boy."

Zoë nodded, her eyes damp with tears of joy. "Our little boy. I like that."

"Me, too."

Together, they stood and walked outside. The wind rustled the trees overhead. Yellow-and-red leaves littered the front lawn as Tanner held her hand and led her down the path to the driveway.

His truck sat parked along the street in front of her house. As he opened the door to let her in, she glanced at the left front fender and paused. "The scratches are gone."

He wrapped an arm around her shoulders and spoke low. "I got them repaired. I hope you don't mind. I figured it was time to let the past go and start a new beginning."

"Yes, it certainly is."

And that was exactly what they did.

Epilogue

Fifteen months later

"Mom! Dad! I caught one."

Zoë turned and looked at Jonah. The boy stood on the dock at Kids' Creek Park, the afternoon sun gleaming against his golden head. His fishing pole arched slightly as a fish tugged on the line. Jonah turned the reel, pulled, then released, setting the hook in the fish's mouth just as Tanner had taught him. At almost eight years of age, Jonah didn't need anyone's help now, but it was thrilling to watch him work.

"I'm coming," Zoë called.

Stepping over the slippery stones by the

shore, she held out both hands to catch herself in case she stumbled. She felt so heavy and cumbersome. But then she found Tanner's strong arm around her thick waist and she relaxed.

"You're always near when I need you," she said.

"I don't want you to fall and hurt my two babies," he spoke low against her ear, his warm breath fanning her cheek.

A shiver of delight ran up her spine. She lifted a hand to her distended middle, feeling the rigorous movements of their child within her. "I'm only having one baby. And the sooner the better. I can't even see my feet, much less tie my shoes anymore. I'm tired of being pregnant."

He chuckled. "At almost nine months, I don't blame you. But you'll always be my baby, too."

She leaned against his solid strength, letting him help her walk up the muddy slope. Actually, he walked and she waddled, glaring at the ducks as they bobbled along beside her. She knew exactly how they felt.

Tanner escorted her over to the dock where they watched Jonah net a five-inch trout. Jonah unhooked the thrashing fish and held it gently in his hands, his lips pursed as he eyed its scrawny size with disgust. "What do you think, Dad? Too small?"

Tanner shrugged. "It's up to you, son. But it could use another year's growth, that's for sure."

Without a word, Jonah tossed the little fish back into the pond. With a flip of its tail, it disappeared among the tall grasses jutting upward along the banks. Jonah then stepped over to Zoë and rubbed her baby tummy.

"Don't worry, sis, I'll catch us a bigger fish next time."

The boy raced off to another spot on the other side of the pond. Opening the tackle box, he reached for a new piece of deli shrimp, attached it to the hook and tossed his line back into the water. A satisfied smile curved his lips, and he appeared contented and secure in his life.

The way a little boy ought to be.

Watching her son, Zoë couldn't believe how grown-up he'd become in such a short time. So confident and sure of himself. "He sure is happy to be having a little sister to show off for. He's becoming a fishing pro, just like you."

Tanner wrapped his arms around her from behind, resting his hands over the top of her stomach. "He'll make a wonderful big brother."

She turned to her husband, cuddling her face close within the crook of his warm throat. She breathed deeply of his spicy scent, thinking there was nowhere on earth she'd rather be. Two years earlier, she never would have believed she and Jonah could be so happy. So content. And it was all because Tanner refused to give up on them. Now they were a real family. And with God's grace, they'd have this new baby and possibly more in the future.

The Lord had truly blessed them, working a miracle on their behalf. And each morning as Zoë arose, she promised herself she'd never take her beloved family for granted again.

"I agree, he will make a sweet big brother. You're the best father I could ever give my children," she whispered.

"And you're the best mother I can give to mine. I love you, sweetheart."

"And I love you."

As Tanner kissed her, she released a deep sigh of happiness. Other than a healthy baby, she couldn't ask for anything more.

* * * * *

Dear Reader,

Saving an endangered species of fish might not seem like a compelling topic for an inspirational romance, but after researching this book, I discovered how everything we do can impact a myriad of ecosystems in the most amazing ways.

I believe that we have a loving Heavenly Father who prepared this beautiful earth for our use. He wants us to utilize this planet's resources for our good, but not to excess. And not without serious thought about the ramifications of our actions. When we abuse the earth and make no contingency plan for it to heal, we abuse the wonderful gifts God has given us.

In *Falling for the Forest Ranger,* both the hero and heroine are fighting to repair the damage done by mankind to the rivers and streams in a small part of Idaho. Their work methods differ, but their goals are the same. As they try to repair the earth, they are able to heal their own broken hearts and find joy in God's redeeming love. We all are a part of this earth and God's creation. He wants us to be happy. He is very aware of each and every one of us, just as He is aware of every fish, flower, rock and creature on the earth. Not only should we be good stewards of the earth, but we should also have gratitude for what the Lord has given us.

I hope you enjoy reading *Falling for the Forest Ranger* and I invite you to visit my website at www.LeighBale.com to learn more about my books.

May you find peace in the Lord's words!
Leigh Bale

Questions for Discussion

1. In *Falling for the Forest Ranger,* Zoë Lawton is a widow raising a young son on her own. She worked hard to support her child while finishing her education, yet she feels grateful to the Lord for providing a way for her to accomplish these tasks. Do you think Zoë should have stayed home and lived off welfare instead of striving to earn her own living and take care of herself? Why or why not?

2. Tanner Bohlman is an intelligent, educated man who was desperately hurt when his fiancée broke off their engagement just weeks before they were to be married. Having been raised in foster care, he has lived most of his life alone. Have you ever been hurt by love before? If so, how did you handle it? Did you give up on loving again? Or did you hold tight to your faith that

you would find someone else one day? Why or why not?

3. Paul Carter is a member of Zoë's congregation. He's been divorced a couple of times and has two sons by different mothers. He bluntly confesses that he doesn't like the kids, yet he likes the women until they become "too clingy." Do you know any men or women who are frequently in and out of romantic relationships, yet they never seem to genuinely care about their children or spouses? Why do you think this is? What might they do to change this and bless the lives of their children?

4. Once Tanner finally returns to church, he is surprised by the warm welcome he receives from complete strangers as well as people he already knows. Have you ever welcomed someone you didn't know? Has a stranger welcomed you? Why is it important for us to go out of our way to welcome

people into our church family? How can we overcome our shyness to offer others a welcoming hand?

5. Once Tanner confides to Zoë that his fiancée broke his heart and married his best friend, Zoë points out that it is good that Tanner didn't marry the woman. Zoë is glad the other couple found love and happiness together. Tanner never thought of it that way. He realizes that if he really loved his fiancée the way he should love a woman he wants to marry, he should be glad she is happy. This opens Tanner's heart to forgiveness and he finally wishes her well. He would not want to marry a woman who loves someone else. Have you ever had your heart broken but then been glad that the other person found happiness with someone else? Do you think this is good or bad? Do you think this is part of the healing process? Why or why not?

6. During their kayaking trip, Zoë quickly learns to follow Tanner's hand signals as he indicates less hazardous paths she should take on the white water. She never hesitates to take his direction, trusting him completely as she follows his commands without question. How can we school ourselves to trust the Lord in the same way? Should we hesitate before obeying God's commandments? Sometimes it's hard to obey without question, but will we be happier in the end if we do? Why or why not? Will keeping God's commandments and obeying His will ensure we never have difficulties or pain in our lives? Why or why not?

7. Tanner harbors anger and hurt toward God for taking away everyone he's ever loved. Do you think Tanner's anger is justified? If so, how much time should pass before Tanner forgives and forgets? Why or why not?

8. When Tanner is badly injured on a kayaking trip with Zoë, she is reminded of the time when she held her husband after a bad skiing accident that took his life. She fears losing another man she loves. Have you ever been in a drastic situation over which you had no control? Did you panic or maintain control until the tragedy was over? How can exercising faith and prayer help us deal with traumatic situations?

9. After Tanner realizes that he loves Zoë, he still fears telling her his true feelings. He knows there are no guarantees she'll never hurt him or that they'll always be happy together. Are there any guarantees in life? Why or why not? How can we face life's trials with faith and courage?

10. Blaine Milan is a loving father and husband, and strong in his faith. He sets a good example for Tanner and is the kind of man he'd like to be. Has

anyone in your life set a good example for you? Did you try to follow that example, or did you end up giving up on the effort? Why?

11. After her husband's death, Zoë worked hard in school to build a career for herself so she could take care of herself and her young child. Later, when Tanner asks her to give up her job in Portland to be with him, she can't bring herself to abandon the security of her good job. It takes nearly losing Tanner before she realizes that even the security of her career is not more important than love. Do you agree with her? Why or why not?

12. Have you ever been faced with losing your home and livelihood? How did it make you feel? When we lose the comforts of life, how can we exercise faith and trust in God to keep us safe?

13. Having lost every person he ever loved, Tanner has been alone most of

his life. Do you think he is wise to protect his heart from being hurt again? Why or why not?

14. Tanner finally comes to realize that life is hard and full of uncertainties. There are no guarantees, except that God loves us and will never desert us even in our darkest hour. Knowing this, do you think it should make us more cautious or more courageous in living our lives? Why?

REQUEST YOUR FREE BOOKS!

2 FREE INSPIRATIONAL NOVELS IN TRUE LARGE PRINT
PLUS 2 FREE MYSTERY GIFTS

Love Inspired™

TRUE LARGE PRINT

YES! Please send me 2 FREE Love Inspired® True Large Print novels and my 2 FREE mystery gifts (gifts are worth about $10). After receiving them, if I don't wish to receive any more books, I can return the shipping statement marked "cancel." If I don't cancel, I will receive 3 brand-new true large print novels every month and be billed just $7.99 per book in the U.S. or $9.99 per book in Canada. That's a savings of at least 33% off the cover price. It's quite a bargain! Shipping and handling is just 50¢ per book in the U.S. and 75¢ per book in Canada.* I understand that accepting the 2 free books and gifts places me under no obligation to buy anything. I can always return the shipment and cancel at any time. Even if I never buy another book, the two free books and gifts are mine to keep forever.

117/307 IDN FVZK

Name _____ (PLEASE PRINT)

Address _____ Apt. #

City _____ State/Prov. _____ Zip/Postal Code

Signature (if under 18, a parent or guardian must sign)

Mail to the Harlequin® Reader Service:
IN U.S.A.: P.O. Box 1867, Buffalo, NY 14240-1867
IN CANADA: P.O. Box 609, Fort Erie, Ontario L2A 5X3

* Terms and prices subject to change without notice. Prices do not include applicable taxes. Sales tax applicable in N.Y. Canadian residents will be charged applicable taxes. Offer not valid in Quebec. This offer is limited to one order per household. Not valid for current subscribers to Love Inspired True Large Print books. All orders subject to credit approval. Credit or debit balances in a customer's account(s) may be offset by any other outstanding balance owed by or to the customer. Please allow 4 to 6 weeks for delivery. Offer available while quantities last.

Your Privacy—The Harlequin® Reader Service is committed to protecting your privacy. Our Privacy Policy is available online at www.ReaderService.com or upon request from the Harlequin Reader Service.

We make a portion of our mailing list available to reputable third parties that offer products we believe may interest you. If you prefer that we not exchange your name with third parties, or if you wish to clarify or modify your communication preferences, please visit us at www.ReaderService.com/consumerchoice or write to us at Harlequin Reader Service Preference Service, P.O. Box 9062, Buffalo, NY 14269. Include your complete name and address.

LITLP13TR

ReaderService.com

Manage your account online!

- Review your order history
- Manage your payments
- Update your address

---

*We've designed
the Harlequin® Reader Service
website just for you.*

Enjoy all the features!

- Reader excerpts from any series
- Respond to mailings and special monthly offers
- Discover new series available to you
- Browse the Bonus Bucks catalogue
- Share your feedback

Visit us at:

ReaderService.com